Schobert

Flashing Swords!
#2

FLASHING SWORDS!
#2

Edited, with an Introduction
and Notes, by
LIN CARTER

NELSON DOUBLEDAY, Inc.
Garden City, New York

Published by arrangement with
Dell Publishing Co., Inc.
750 Third Avenue
New York, N.Y. 10017

Printed in the United States of America

This second volume of
Flashing Swords!
is dedicated with love
and admiration to the late
HENRY KUTTNER
one of the best Swordsmen
and Sorcerers of 'em all

Contents

THE INTRODUCTION:

Flashing Swords and Black Magicians

You HAVE never read any of the stories in this book before, because they are all brand-new ones, written especially for this second volume of *Flashing Swords!;* and herein you will find a new "Elric" yarn by Michael Moorcock, a new "Witch World" novelette by Andre Norton, a new "Pusâdian" tale by L. Sprague de Camp, and a new "Brak the Barbarian" story by John Jakes.

These four 15,000-worders are splendid examples of an exciting "new" kind of fantasy fiction known to its *aficionados* as "Sword & Sorcery." Although the term itself, in obvious analogy with "cloak and dagger," "thud and blunder" and similar labels, was coined by fantasy writer Fritz Leiber, the school of fiction which bears the name was invented by Robert E. Howard.

ROBERT E. (for Ervin) Howard was an energetic and very successful pulp-fiction writer, born in 1906 in the town of Peaster, Texas, who spent most of his unhappily brief life in Cross Plains, which is in the center of Texas between Brownwood and Abilene, and who died there in 1936.

Howard founded the *genre* of Sword & Sorcery in 1932. In December of that year, an issue of a popular horror fiction magazine called *Weird Tales* was published containing a story by him entitled "The Phoenix on the Sword." That particular story introduced a brawling barbarian adventurer, one Conan of Cimmeria, and a gorgeous, glittering world that might have, certainly should have but unfortunately did not exist *circa* 15,000 B.C., in that shadowy and mythic age between the destruction of Atlantis and the birth of Egypt and Chaldea.

"The Phoenix on the Sword" was not just an adventure story, although it had excitement and color enough for any two yarns. It had the element of fantasy—magic, sorcery, the supernatural—and the added ingredient of horror. This last element was a requirement, more or less, of the publisher. *Weird Tales* would take an occasional bit of fantasy, or adventure, or even humor, but the magazine was built on modern-day ghost stories, and horror must be present.

It was a popular story, and the editor, Farnsworth Wright, wanted to see more. Howard happily complied. He had tried twice before to sell Farnsworth Wright on the idea of a series of short fiction about the adventures of one or another hero. In the late 1920's he had fired off to *WT* a heap of tales about an Atlantean savage named Kull; Wright bought only two and fired the rest straight back to Cross Plains. Then he had tried to place a slender bundle of yarns about a Prince of the Picts named Bran Mak Morn and his struggles against the Roman legions; alas, Farnsworthy the Finnicky liked them no better. But Conan was something else again: the hero had character and personality and stature, and the story settings (i.e., a whole prehistoric Europe, Africa and Asia) had variety and exotic charm.

Not knowing he had only four years left to live, Howard settled down to creating his Conan saga. During the next year—1933—Conan was all over *Weird Tales*. The January issue contained "The Scarlet Citadel"; in March "The Tower of the Elephant" appeared; the June issue featured "Black Colossus"; "The Slithering Shadow" was published in September; and the October issue had "The Pool of the Black One."

The readers ate it up and wanted more. In 1934 *Weird Tales* printed five more Conan short stories, a three-part novella, and, with the December issue, began serialization of the only full-length Conan novel Howard ever wrote, *The Hour of the Dragon*. More Conan filled the magazine during 1935, and in the issues for July through October 1936 appeared the last of the Conan stories, "Red Nails." It is probable that Howard did not ever see it in print, for at eight o'clock on the hot summer morning of July 11, 1936, in a mood of black depression over the death of his mother, Robert Ervin Howard put a pistol to his head and blew his brains out.

VERY few writers are privileged to do something truly new and different. Most writers (myself included) merely contribute new work to a school or movement or *genre* begun by someone else. Howard was one of the gifted few.

No one had ever before quite written fiction like his Conan stories. Oh, sure, you can trace the indomitable barbarian warrior hero back to Siegfried, or the theme of the hero battling hand to hand against the forces of supernatural evil back to Beowulf's tussel with Grendel or Saint George's duel with the dragon, if you like. The basic elements—the raw materials of Sword & Sorcery, if you will—have been floating around loose in literature for millennia. But it is to Howard's lasting credit that he alone was first to nail them down and put them together in the proper proportion, balance and tension.

Conan emerged as the most popular series character in that decade of *Weird Tales*. The faithful readership grieved over Howard's untimely death: but they were hungry for more of the same. And if they could not get more genuine original Conan, they were willing to devour ersatz Conan.

Thus Sword & Sorcery became, not just one author's own private province, but a real *genre*. Even before Howard's death, new writers had eagerly tried their hand at Sword & Sorcery. The very first of these was a young lady who wrote under the name of C. L. Moore; she conceived of a novel twist on the Howardian school, and came up with a *female* Conan named Jirel of Joiry, who first appeared in a story entitled "The Black God's Kiss" in the October 1934 *Weird Tales*. (By a lovely coincidence, the second part of one of Howard's serialized Conan stories, "People of the Black Circle," was published in that same issue.)

While the Jirel stories were still running in *WT*, another writer, Clifford Ball, turned his hand to the young *genre*, his first S&S yarn, "Duar the Accursed," appearing in the issue of May 1937. And the following year a young free-lance writer named Henry Kuttner launched an excellent series of his own with a tale called "Thunder in the Dawn," a two-part serial which ran in the issues of May and June 1938. No grim, silent barbarian, Kuttner's character was a suave and witty daredevil Atlantean prince, Elak. Kuttner broadened the *genre* with the notion that a hero deserves a sidekick, and Elak and his roguish comrade, Lycon, encountered in that story a Druid, a primal god who lived at the bottom of a pool, a witch-girl, a semi-human race and assorted other perils. (Parenthetically, Kuttner was to marry Catherine Moore in 1940.)

By this time the school had spread even to other magazines. *WT*'s only real competitor for the fantasy audience was Street & Smith's *Unknown*. In 1939, while *WT* was still running Jirel and Elak stories, *Unknown* introduced a new character, Wan Tengri, in a short novel called *Flame Winds* by Norvell W. Page. And, in *Unknown* for August 1939, appeared a tale called "Two Sought Adventure," by Fritz Leiber, the first of many Sword & Sorcery stories featuring a lovable pair of swashbuckling rogues named Fafhrd and the Gray Mouser—a series, incidentally, that is *still* running (although not, alas, in *Unknown*, which succumbed to the paper shortage in World War II).

WHILE only eighteen Conan stories were published during Howard's lifetime, it was discovered years later that he had written or begun very many others. A latecomer to the *genre*, L. Sprague de Camp, discovered what turned out to be the first of several caches of previously unknown and unpublished Howard manuscripts, when in 1951 he turned up a box of typescript in the apartment of a man who had been Howard's literary agent. Some of these stories were complete, some only rough drafts, some fragments. Edited and sometimes completed by de Camp, these newly discovered Conan stories began appearing in various magazines during the early 1950's. In 1965 the first of what would eventually become a twelve-volume set of the *complete* Conan appeared in paperback from Lancer Books; it includes all of the Conan stories in correct order, the new stories fitted in where they belong, with some of the larger gaps in the saga filled by new pastiches written by L. Sprague de Camp and myself. As of this writing, *twenty-two* new Conan stories have been added to Howard's original eighteen, including three new book-length novels.

Beyond Howard, Moore, Ball, Kuttner, Page and Leiber, other new writers have come along to work in the Conan tradition. Some of these are L. Sprague de Camp, who, besides editing the Howardian manuscripts and collaborating with me on new pastiches, has launched a series of his own "Pusâdian" tales, set in a fresh, original conception of Atlantis; John Jakes, whose "Brak the Barbarian," frankly modeled on the doughty Cimmerian, is the hero of a cycle of fine yarns still going strong; myself, with a series of (so far) six paperback novels of the wanderings and adventures of Thongor the Mighty, barbarian hero-king of Lost Lemuria; Andre Norton, who turned from authoring popular teen-age science fiction adventures to create a distinguished series of novels for adult enthusiasts, the excellent "Witch World" books; and a talented young Britisher, Michael Moorcock, whose "Elric" stories have won an enthusiastic following.

ONLY a few years ago it occurred to us that we should organize a writers' guild composed *exclusively* of Sword & Sorcery specialists. A club with the pretentious name of "The Swordsmen and Sorcerers' Guild of America, Ltd." ("SAGA" for short) was soon formed, with de Camp, Jakes and Carter as founding fathers. Fritz Leiber, Mike Moorcock, and Jack Vance, were the next trio elected to swell our far-flung ranks, and the most recent members are Poul Anderson and Andre Norton.

The original idea behind SAGA (quite refreshingly different from *other* clubs like the Science Fiction Writers of America or the Mystery Writers of America) was to have a guild that does absolutely nothing. *No* officers, committees, publications, annual dinners, awards, crusades, blacklists, dues, tithes or weregild. Like all such good ideas, this one has been stretched a little in actual practice.

Two years ago at a science fiction convention in St. Louis, it chanced to occur to one of us—no one quite remembers which one —that, with all the mind-croggling Talent in our ranks, we should (with an eye on the healthy commercial success of all-new annual science fiction anthologies like Damon Knight's *Orbit* series) launch an "official" SAGA anthology to which each of our eight brilliant literary craftsman-type members would contribute a new story, splitting the loot therefrom evenly.

A publisher was located who found this notion to his liking, a title was coined, and, all of the SAGAmen being agreeable to the task, the result is in your hands now.

This book, *Flashing Swords! #2*, is the companion volume to a tome aptly entitled *Flashing Swords! #1*. *#1* contains a new "Fafhrd and the Gray Mouser" tale by Fritz Leiber, a new "Dying Earth" yarn by Jack Vance, a new "Viking Age" swashbuckler by the redoubtable Poul Anderson, and a new story (first in a series) about Amalric the Mangod of Thoorana by the undersigned. If you enjoy the contents of the book you are now reading, I direct your attention to its companion volume, also on the stands right now.

And—*Flashing Swords! #3*?
We'll have to see about that . . .

LIN CARTER

Hollis, Long Island, New York

Flashing Swords!
#2

. . . in Our lands be beeres and Lyons of dyvers colours as ye redd, grene, black, and white. And in Our land be also Unicornes and these Unicornes slee many Lyons.

Also there dare no Man make a lye in Our lande, for if he dyde he sholde incontynent be sleyn.

The Epistle of Prester John, Lord of the Three Indias, to the Monarchs and Emperors of Christiandom

Lost Atlantis has fascinated many fantasy writers, among them Clark Ashton Smith, Henry Kuttner and Howard himself. More recently it has appealed to England's Jane Gaskell and our own L. Sprague de Camp.

Sprague is what we Sword & Sorcery writers ought to be but seldom are. He can ride and shoot and knows the fine points of swordplay. He is an inveterate globetrotter, conversant with many lands and tongues and cultures. He is deeply read in history, archaeology, the occult sciences, literature and myth. Over six feet tall, straight as a ramrod, he has black magnetic eyes, a crisp graying beard, a deep resonant voice and a commanding manner. He is also, of course, a brilliant writer—deft, witty, ironic.

Whereas the rest of us romanticize about ancient Troy and Carthage, the enigmatic ruins of Zimbabwe and Ponape, and mysterious Mayan cities lost in the trackless jungles of Yucatan, Sprague has really been there and has usually written a book about it.

Born in New York in 1907, L. Sprague de Camp was one of the most popular and talented of the small circle of writers for John W. Campbell's *Astounding Science Fiction* and *Unknown* in the 1940's. It is because of de Camp and the others—Asimov, Heinlein, van Vogt, Leiber and one or two more—that the decade is known in the history of modern imaginative fiction as "the *Golden* Forties."

While in recent years Sprague has done much in the line of nonfiction and the historical novel, the best of his early work was fantasy. With Fletcher Pratt he wrote *The Carnelian Cube, Land of*

Unreason, The Incomplete Enchanter, Castle of Iron—books that stand high on everyone's list of the best fantasy of the 1940's. On his own he wrote *The Undesired Princess, Solomon's Stone, Lest Darkness Fall* and (more recently) *The Tritonian Ring* and *The Goblin Tower.*

His accomplishments are too numerous to list in this small space. But he is responsible for bringing the Conan books into paperback and to the attention of millions of readers, not only because of having edited and organized and completed them, besides writing pastiches to flesh out the series, but because of his tireless championing of the merits of Sword & Sorcery in general and Howard's kind in particular.

To get back to Atlantis, Sprague's best book, the most interesting and permanently valuable of them all, is to my taste his encyclopedic study *Lost Continents: The Atlantis Theme in History, Science and Literature* (recently reissued by Dover). This remarkable tome sums up the evidence for and against such legendary civilizations in a manner exhaustive, authoritative and spectacularly entertaining. His conclusion was that Plato was just spinning a good yarn.

Luckily this sobering conclusion that Atlantis never was has not deterred Sprague from spinning some good yarns about Atlantis himself. For fictional purposes Sprague visualizes Atlantis as part of the primal Afro-European continent, centering in the region of the Atlas Mountains, while he locates "Pusâd" (his name for Poseidonis) as a large offshore island where the Azores are now found. This is the general locale of the heroic fantasy novel *The Tritonian Ring* and of several shorter Pusâdian tales, of which this is the newest and, just possibly, the best.

2

The Rug and The Bull

by L. SPRAGUE DE CAMP

1

A PAIR of matched roans, lean from long, hard driving, pulled the two-wheeled post chaise cantering along the road on the right bank of the Baitis. A cloud of yellow dust hung in the still, dry air behind the carriage. The road was lined by huge old cork oaks, planted for shade under King Asizhen long before.

The driver, a big, powerful man in that comfortable stretch between youth and middle age, sat braced on the front seat against the bounces of the vehicle. Now and then he leaned forward to speak to the horses and sometimes to flick them lightly with his whip. Although he never struck them hard, they minded him well enough.

"Zhanes!" he called back over his shoulder. "See if the demon bird be still there."

A boy of thirteen thrust his head out the rear of the carriage. At the sight of a vulture hanging in the sky, a bowshot behind the carriage and an equal distance above it, the boy said: "He's there all right, Dad."

"If you'd lash those beasts smartly," said the woman in the chaise, "we could escape that evil creature."

"Now, darling," said the man, "we've been all over that. Had you been driving, you'd have flogged them to a lathering gallop until they dropped dead, and then Larentius Alba's bravos would have cut all our throats ere we'd cleared Ausonia. As it is, we've kept ahead of them for hundreds of leagues; and Larentius cannot control his familiar at an infinite distance."

"He's turned back, Dad," said the boy as the vulture wheeled and soared off to eastward.

"There you are," said the man.

"He's turned back before and then come on again," said the woman. "He'll fly back to Larentius' cutthroats, to show them the way, and then return to his post."

"We shall see," said the man, checking the horses to a trot and then to a walk.

The man was Gezun of Lorsk, wandering mage and adventurer. He was much taller than the local Euskerians, with a brown skin and abundant curly, glossy-black hair and beard. The hair had receded a little from his forehead, and the beard was shot with a few gray hairs around the chin. He had a broad forehead, beetling brows, a big, sharp nose, wide cheekbones, and a massive square jaw. At his side hung a big cut-and-thrust bronze sword, which rattled in its scabbard as the carriage took the bumps.

Gezun leaned back to speak to his family. "Look, Ro! 'Twas up yonder valley that I took that dame I abducted—she who preferred old Derezong's soft cushions to my hot young virility." He laughed. "Now that I'm past the first flush of youth myself, I can better under-

4

stand her view. If she hadn't, belike you'd never have had me for a husband, and wouldn't that have been doleful fate?"

"Sometimes I wonder," said Gezun's wife. She was a small woman, as dark as Gezun, and pretty in a sharp-featured, birdlike way. She came from mystic Typhon, far to the east in the land of Setesh. "Betimes I weary of this wandering life, ever one leap ahead of vengeful rivals and cheated creditors."

"Now, darling, begin not that song again! As the philosopher Goishek says, one might as well take things as they come, for how else can one take them? Once we shall have made our fortune in Torrutseish, we'll settle down, pay all our debts, and—"

"Curse of the green hippopotamus! I've heard it all before—in Kheru, in Yavan, in Gomer, in Ausonia, in Maxia, and in other places I cannot even recall."

"Not before the children, pray!"

"Oh, go ahead, Daddy!" said the girl Mnera, ten. "When you and Mommy quarrel, we learn such interesting things about your past."

"Conniving wench!" growled Gezun.

"When do we get to Torrutseish?" asked the boy Ugaph, seven.

"Disturb your father not," said Ro. "He needs all his wits to plan his next great exploit. Doubtless he'll sell the king a plan for a floating bridge to the moon."

"Why, darling!" said Gezun, grinning. "What an idea! I misdoubt I can use it in its present form, but something might be made of it—"

"Oh, stop your eternal jesting!"

"I jest not. Forsooth, your proposal is not too far from my own plans for the Carpet of Khazi."

"Seriously," said Ro, "if in sooth the Tartessians be such casteproud snobs, how will you get within shouting distance of King Norskezhek?"

"I have that all planned: a letter of introduction from the chief of the Ausonian magicians' guild to his equivalent in Torrutseish.

5

Magicians move through all levels of society—even so caste-bound a society as that of the Tartessian Empire—like an eel through a thicket of pond lilies."

"But—but—" cried Ro, "the head of the Ausonian magicians is that same Larentius Alba who sent his troop of henchmen to slay us! How came you by a recommendation from him?"

"True, Larentius and I parted on unfriendly terms. But why thought you I spent so much effort in mastering Ausonian writing? Though my glyphs be less than perfect, 'tis unlikely that anyone in Torrutseish will have the knowledge to correct 'em."

"Another forgery!" sighed Ro. "Methinks you'd best make your long deferred killing soon, else you'll run out of countries wherein to make it."

"The world is wide, my sweetheart, and folk forget old grudges with the years."

"Indeed?" began Ro in a disputatious tone. But the boy Zhanes asked:

"Dad, what was it that so provoked Larentius against you? You promised to tell us when we were well away."

Gezun chuckled. "I was fain to buy the Carpet of Khazi from him, for what seemed a fair price, taking into account the fact that he knew not the formulas for magicking it." He glanced back to the interior of the carriage, where the rug, rolled and tied with string, lay among the family's other possessions. "Well, you know how those things go: One makes an offer. T'other says, ridiculous! and sets his price. The one says, 'tis absurd, but raises his own offer by a fingernail paring, and so on. We'd come within bowshot of each other but seemed reluctant to approach nigher, when Larentius proposed that we end the haggle by a game of sacred way, my last offer against the rug. I agreed, but then the scum enchanted the dice—"

"How knew you?" said Mnera.

"What sort of wizard should I be if I did not? When I taxed Larentius with deception, he flew into a rage and threatened me with dire dooms. In sooth, he'd begun to chant a spell, when I recalled a little spell of my own, which has come in handy more than once." Gezun held up a large fist. "I left him in a swoon and came away with the cursed carpet, which I should have won anyhow but for the ensorcelment of his knucklebones."

"You should have slain him whilst you had the chance," said Ro.

"I know, but he looked so old and helpless, lying there with blood trickling from his nose."

"Your tenderheartedness will be the death of us all yet," she said. "Having left enemies in all the civilized lands we've passed through, have you any foes in Torrutseish?"

"Not really—but let me think. Oh, yes, there was a little wizard named—ah—Bokarri, that was it. He wasn't much of a magician, but he sought to swindle me out of a ring of star-metal, which was a sure specific against maleficent magics."

"What befell?"

"'Twas the same as with Larentius Alba; a stout buffet cut athwart his spell ere he could finish it, and I fled with the ring."

"Where's the ring now?"

Gezun sighed. "Ah me, I lost it in Maxia to a shrewder colleague. Forsooth, I was young and foolish then."

"And now you're middle-aged and foolish. But what about this Bokarri? Will he lie in wait for you?"

"I think not. He was much older than I, so by now he's probably joined the majority—unless he's one of those who by celibacy and other austerities has extended his life beyond its wonted span. They say a magician of the highest degree can do so, and so my former master Sancheth Sar claimed to have done. But I suspect that such a joyless life merely *seems* longer.

"We need not, howsomever, worry about Master Bokarri. He was always a third-rate sorcerer who let all the craftier spirits of his stable escape, leaving a few halfwitted spooks of little use. If he have survived, he's probably an old beggar."

7

Hours later the boy Zhanes reported, "There's still no vulture, Dad."

"Ha! Said I not so?" said Gezun. "Methinks the demon spy has reached the boundary beyond which his master forbade him to go, lest he escape altogether from governance. Or else the protective spells that the wizards of Torrutseish cast about their city have held him back, as a weir holds back a fish."

Peering past his father's massive form, the boy Ugaph cried: "There's the city! Look!"

Ahead in the dusty distance rose the vast circular wall of Torrutseish—capital of the Tartessian Empire—on its island in the river Baitis. The wall was of red, white, and black stones arranged in bands and patterns to give a dazzling effect. The bright Euskerian sun gleamed on the gilding of dome and spire and tourelle, and flags bearing the owl of Tartessia flapped in the breeze. The river, which divided and flowed past the city on both sides, swarmed with dugouts, rafts of inflated skins, and other fresh-water craft.

In the foreground rose a wooden structure, circular like the city behind it but on a much smaller scale. Ugaph asked:

"Be that the bull ring, whereof you've told us?"

"It looks like it," said Gezun. "Meseems they've built a new one since I was here last."

"When was that?" asked Ugaph.

Gezun was occupied with paying toll for the pontoon bridge that led to the island. As the wheels of the carriage boomed on the planks of the bridge, he answered his son:

"Ere any of you were born, nearly twenty years ago. The general aspect of mighty Torrutseish hasn't changed. This floating bridge is new, though. In my day we had to take a ferry raft."

"Will you take us to a bullfight, Dad?" said Zhanes.

Gezun made a sour face. "Now wherefore should you wish to attend so cruel spectacle, where men at little risk to themselves tease a noble aurochs till the beast be stark worn out and then spear him so as to vaunt themselves great heroes?"

8

"We would see it for the excitement, Dad," said Zhanes. "Oh, please, take us to a bullfight!"

"You promised, back in Ausonia," said the younger boy.

Ro said, "Some of your oddities, Gezun, I've gotten used to in the last fifteen years. But I shall never understand this mad notion that men should be kind to animals—*animals*, mind you!"

The boys continued to goad and cajole Gezun until at last he said, "Very well, I will take you to a bullfight at the first opportunity. But once only, mind! I would not have you develop a taste for the bloody business."

Then he drew rein before the East Gate of Torrutseish and prepared to identify himself to the guards.

2

INSIDE the gate the streets swarmed with the variegated throng that any metropolis attracts. Most were the native Euskerians in tight breeches, black mantles, and little round black caps. There were also sprinklings of Kerneans in robes and Kaffias, with rings in their ears; refined-looking Hesperians in blue-and-white cloaks and tunics; towering Pusâdians in tartan kilts and cloaks; reddish-blond Atlanteans in vermilion-dyed goatskins; gaping Galathan barbarians with checkered trews and drooping mustaches; slender black Gamphasants from the far South; and many others.

At the Guildhall a handsomely clad Gezun asked the ostiary, "Tell me, pray, when and where meets the local magicians' guild?"

"On the night of the full moon, sir, in the Charter Room—the third on the right as you ascend the stair."

"When and where is the president of the guild to be found?"

"He's in the Charter Room of evenings, each sennight following the monthly meeting. Tonight's one of his nights."

"I thank you," said Gezun. Turning to Ro, he said, "We have some hours ere I needs must come back here. Meanwhile, we can seek permanent quarters to rent and buy some furnishings."

That evening, leaving his family—exhausted from shopping and moving furniture—in their new house, Gezun returned to the Guildhall. He found the Charter Room and knocked.

"Come in!" said a creaky old voice.

Gezun entered. By the light of several rushlights, Gezun saw, at the end of a long table, a small, skinny oldster, with a narrow, vulpine face and straggly white hair. He was seated at a pile of parchments and reed papers, on which he was working. The man looked up.

"Good even, fair sir," said Gezun. "I have but now arrived in your splendid city and would pay my respects to my wizardly colleagues."

The old man, after peering at Gezun from under white eyebrows, left his seat and came around the table, holding up a rushlight the better to see Gezun's face. He said:

"Have I not met you before? Your face recalls—but then, tell me your name, young man, and save me some tedious guessing."

"Gezun of Lorsk, sir. I have here a letter of introduction from—"

"*Gezun?* Fry my balls! Not the same Gezun who was in Torrutseish a score of years ago? That young hoodlum?"

"Well—ah—sir—"

The old man's voice rose to a shriek. "Know you me not? Behold, I am Bokarri, whom you foully robbed! I'll do for thee this time, thou son of a barren sow! Thou dung-eating maggot! Thou flea's pizzle! *Avratamon garish hva ungorix—*"

"Wait, wait!" yelled Gezun. "Ere you cast a spell, wouldn't you like the debt you think I owe you repaid?"

Bokarri broke off, staring. "What's this?"

10

"Look. We parted on, let's say, strained terms, eighteen years ago, did we not?"

"That were a prize understatement. But go on."

"And meseems we disputed the ownership of a certain iron ring, yes?"

"Aye, albeit your claim was but a tissue of lies and bluff."

"That's as may be. It seemed sound to me—now, wait, no more unseemly rages, pray! Let's agree that each of us thought he owned the bauble."

"Can you now return me this bauble, as you call it? Or pay me the talent of gold 'tis worth?"

"A talent? Oh, come, sir, you jest!"

"Prices have risen. The trade-metal changers call it inflation. Have you the ring?"

"Nay, alas. I lost it in Maxia, somewhat as you lost it to me."

"What, then? Art willing to be my slave till death us do part?"

"Nay again, good my master. But I can put you in the way of many times the value of the ring by joining me in a certain enterprise."

Bokarri chewed his scanty whiskers. "I prefer cash to any vagabond's moon-dreams."

"The cash I have not, sir; but, when you hear my scheme, you'll deem yourself the luckiest thaumaturge west of Kheru."

"I'd sooner believe that the sun will rise in the west tomorrow; but speak."

"Have you ever heard of the Carpet of Khazi?"

"Oh, aye. Made by the wizardly weaver Khazi in Typhon, with a demon woven into the very fabric. Him who commands the demon, the carpet will bear through the air like the flight of a bird."

"Well, I have the Carpet of Khazi."

"How came you by it?"

"I obtained it in Ausonia. The owner, not knowing the secret magical tongue of Setesh, could not use the thing, so I got it for a fraction of its true worth."

11

"And know you the magical jargon of Setesh?"

"Aye. I learnt it in partnership with my late father-in-law, the wizard Ugaph, in Typhon. I have practiced with the rug until the demon Yiqqal obeys me as a sheep dog obeys its shepherd."

"Interesting," said Bokarri. "But where's the profit in this thing? True, 'twere useful in escaping one's foes. Did you mean to give it to me, in lieu of the ring?"

"Nay, sir. I—"

"Not that I'd take it. Flying through the air, forsooth! Flay me, but I fear heights, and my old bones are too brittle to endure a tumble. So?"

"The weavers of Torrutseish are the world's most adept. They are not only diligent but also efficient. They organize their work so that one Tartessian weaver can turn out as much carpet in a moon as one of another nation can in a year."

"True. Well, then?"

"My thought is to set up a factory to make carpets like that of Khazi," said Gezun.

"With a separate demon in each one?"

"Why not? I know the method Khazi used, and there are always plenty of demons to be had by a sorcerer who knows how to evoke them. We'll sell a flying carpet to every lordling, magnate, and official in Tartessia, at a stout profit."

"The king would demand control of any enterprise so lucrative," said Bokarri.

"I have thought of that. In any case, we shall need royal backing to set up our factory. You have access to the king, do you not?"

"Certes; and you doubtless wish me to present you to His Majesty and"—Bokarri snorted— "give you a good character."

"Aye, sir."

"Well, we shall see what can be done, albeit 'twill be like trying to whitewash a raven. A fair warning, though: he'll demand the bulk of the profits."

"That surprises me not, from what I've seen of kings. But there should be enough left over to make us both rich."

"Depending on how this surplus be divided. For my part in the scheme I shall naturally expect half."

"Come, Master Bokarri! No introduction is worth that. I can find someone else who has the king's ear. One tenth is what I had in mind."

"Why, you impudent scoundrel . . ."

For an hour they haggled, finally agreeing on one third for Bokarri and two thirds for Gezun. The latter said:

"Now, Master Bokarri, swear by your magical powers that you'll furnish this introduction as promised, without treachery or backbiting."

"I'll swear; but you must likewise swear to fulfill your part of the bargain."

They swore, knowing that a magician who swore falsely by his magical powers lost these powers instanter. Gezun said:

"Tell me, friend Bokarri, how came you to head your guild? No offense intended, but when last I saw you, you were not exactly at the tip-top of your profession."

Bokarri chuckled. "Executive ability, my boy. My colleagues learnt that, although some might surpass me in this or that magical specialty, I alone possessed the knack of keeping a group like this running smoothly, like a well-oiled and well-adjusted water clock."

Gezun thought: he means skill at spying and intrigue. But he did not say so aloud. Instead, he accepted the goblet of the green wine of Zhysk that Bokarri pushed toward him and said:

"My heartfelt thanks, good my sir. The years seem to have entreated you well."

Bokarri shrugged. "By spells and austerities I've been able to stave 'em off a little; but they pile up on all of us soon or late. You do not look starved yourself. Forsooth, methinks I see the beginnings of a potbelly."

"My reserve against want," said Gezun.

"Have a care, or you'll grow as obese as His Majesty."

"I'll bear your warning in mind. Well, here's to Gezun and Bokarri, wizardly weavers extraordinary!"

While waiting for Bokarri to arrange an audience with King Norskezhek, Gezun completed the furnishing of his new house and arranged for his children to attend the school of a local pedagogue. Since they required coaching in the Euskerian language, Gezun had to pay extra. By the time he had done all this, his reserve of trade metal had dwindled alarmingly. Hence he was in no expansive mood when, one afternoon, his boys besought him to take them to a bullfight. Zhanes said:

"The next one is but three days off, Dad, and there won't be another for a month. 'Tis on the festival of Roi, the Tartessian rain god. And you promised to take us to the first one that came up!"

"You promised, Daddy!" Ugaph chimed in.

Gezun defended himself for a time. Then, wearied, he said, "Well, 'tis folly, but I'll tell you. If my colleague Bokarri arrange a definite audience with the king before this bullfight comes off, I'll take you to this polluted spectacle."

"Did you mean to take Mnera and me, too?" said Ro.

"Not exactly—'twere an unseemly spectacle for gentle women—"

"Oh, no, you don't, Gezun! Here, women attend these events as well as men. Think not that your women will be pleased to sit home, sweeping the floor and peeling turnips, whilst you three have all the fun—"

After further argument, Gezun gave in again. "You Seteshan women think you should have rights equal to those of men!"

"And why should we not?" replied Ro.

"Why, did the world adopt so mad a scheme, 'twould mean the utter overthrow and wrack of civilization!"

THE TRUMPET blew, the main gate of the ring opened, and—to the music of the royal military band—the bullfighters deployed into the arena and paraded in ranks and files across the sand. The audience, most of them black-cloaked Euskerians, sent up a cheer.

First came the lancers, afoot and mounted; they slew the bulls. Then came the darters, afoot and mounted; they infuriated the bulls by thrusting darts into their humps. Lastly came a score of chulos, the assistant bullfighters who distracted the bulls with their antics and wore them down.

The leading lancer brought his horse to a stop at the side of the arena opposite to the gate. Squinting against the glare, Gezun made out a royal box, wherein sat a huge fat man in a spangled robe, with a crown on his head. The band fell silent and the marchers halted.

There ensued a half-heard colloquy between the leading lancer and the seated man, with much bowing and polite gestures. "Who's that?" asked Zhanes.

"That's King Norskezhek," said Gezun. "The head bullfighter needs must ask his permission to begin the tauromachy—albeit never in all the centuries of Torrutseish has the king or his deputy withheld it."

Permission granted, the leading lancer led his troop in a circle around the ring, while the band resumed its play. Individual bullfighters waved or called to acquaintances in the crowd. Then all filed out the main gate. A few minutes later the gate opened again and the first bull galloped out.

This was a three-year-old aurochs: big, black, and furious. The beast raced around the ring, head up and nostrils flared, sending the chulos scampering through the gaps in the inner barrier, which were wide enough for them but too narrow for a bull.

"Why is he so angry?" asked Ugaph.

"See you that pair of red and white ribbons that trail from his shoulder hump?" said Gezun. "Ere he's released, they drive a bronzen pin, bearing these ribbons, into his flesh. He, naturally, mislikes the stab of the pin."

The chulos got to work, slipping out from the annular space between the inner and outer barriers and teasing the bull by waving their scarlet cloaks, tempting it to futile charges. Zhanes said:

"Why does the bull always charge the cloak instead of the man? That seems stupid to me."

"Bulls are not very clever," said Gezun.

Presently the bull began to slow down. Its head was no longer held so high. The first of the darters stepped into the ring with his darts in his hands. After he and the bull had circled each other warily for some minutes, the darter leaped forward with a dancing step, just as the bull began a charge. The darter slipped nimbly to one side and planted his darts in the animal's hump. Feeling itself assailed from behind, the bull instantly stopped its charge and circled to find the source of its pain. Thrice more the process was repeated, until the bull had been pierced by eight gaily colored darts—one of which, however, fell out and lay in the sand.

Lastly, a lancer cantered into the ring, bearing a lance with an unusually long, slender, tapering brozen head. The bull, now badly winded and worn, made a sluggish charge at the horse. The rider evaded the charge, and another. Then, as the bull stood with hanging head, the lancer circled round and suddenly charged the bull from its left side, driving his lance into its body just aft of the shoulder. Down went the bull. The audience whooped and cheered. The rider walked his horse around the ring, bowing and waving to vigorous applause.

"This is great, Dad!" cried the boys. But Mnera said, "I don't think it's great at all. 'Tis cruel, as Dad said."

"Sissy!" said Ugaph, and brother and sister fell to pushing and punching each other until forcibly separated.

The second bull was assailed by a mounted darter, who threw his darts at the animal's hump. This bull caught the horse by a sudden charge and overthrew it, ripping open its belly so that its guts gushed out and became entangled with its thrashing legs. Since the rider was pinned under his struggling mount, the chulos rushed out to distract the bull before it could attack the prostrate man. Others pulled the rider free and helped him out of the ring. The dying horse was dragged off by a team of mules.

Another mounted darter took the place of the first. When he had planted all his missiles, and the bull's head hung low from the injury to the muscles of its neck and back, a lancer on foot slew the beast.

The third bull knocked down two chulos, who were rescued by their comrades' fluttering cloaks. Then it leaped over the inner barrier, while the audience voiced its disapproval of this unsportsmanlike conduct by an outburst of whistles and hisses. The bull thundered around the ring-shaped space between the two barriers, while the men standing in this space—soldiers, bullfighters, bull owners, stablemen, and officials of the bull ring—fled madly ahead of it. Soon, however, a movable section of the inner barrier was swung outward gatewise, diverting the animal back into the arena.

This bull proved tough. Even after it had received three lance thrusts in the heart region, it refused to die. Drooling blood from its mouth and nostrils, it walked slowly away from its tormentors until it collapsed.

Zhanes asked, "When does one of the bullfighters get killed?"

"There's no way of telling," said Gezun. "It does happen, but not very often—perhaps once a year."

Mnera said, "I see not why they think themselves such great heroes, then. If as many men as bulls were slain, there would be some point to it."

"I've seen enough bulls killed," said Ugaph. "Now I want to see a man get it."

"Why, you bloodthirsty little devil!" said Gezun.

"You let them talk you into bringing them," said Ro. "If they grow up murderers—"

"I do not see you and Mnera staying home lest the sight contaminate you," said Gezun. "If—"

Just then the fourth bull knocked down a lancer on foot and gored him. The bull was quickly lured away by the chulos, and the man was carried off by his comrades. His injury, however, proved a mere gash over the ribs. Crudely bandaged, he was soon back in the ring and slew his bull, who by now had been so worn down by the chulos that it could do little but stand and await its fate. To frenzied cheers, the lancer strutted around the ring with his bare brown arse showing through the rents in his ripped and bloody costume.

"I've had enough," said Ro.

"So have I," said Mnera.

The boys protested that they wished to remain; but after another bull they, too, agreed to depart. Zhanes said:

"Dad, I've been thinking. These people fix things so it looks terribly dangerous. But really, they've got it arranged so there's only a little danger—much less than a soldier has in any old battle."

"It's just getting steaks the hard way," added Ugaph.

"I'm glad you see it thus," said Gezun. "But say it not to any Tartessian. It would enrage him. They have what they call a 'mystique' about bullfighting. It expresses the dauntless courage of the nation, or some such nonsense."

"But," said Mnera, "the people who come to watch run no risk at all, so where's their dauntless courage? The bull can't jump that outer barrier—"

"Yes, yes, I know," said Gezun, "but now we must gather our gear to go. Have you the picnic basket, Ro?"

4

ON A THRONE of ebony, inlaid with gold and mammoth ivory, sat Norskezhek the Third (also called, but not to his face, Norskezhek the Stout), king of the united Euskerian nations: Tartessia, Turdetania, and Turdulia. The kings of Aremoria, Hesperia, and Phaiaxia paid him tribute. A pair of guards in mail shirts of bronzen scales, with zaghnals or battle picks on their shoulders and double-curved Tartessian swords at their sides, flanked him.

The usher called: "The worthy Master Gezun, traveling wizard!" Gezun strode forward, dropped to both knees, and bowed until his forehead touched the floor. Then, straightening, he asked the usher:

"Have I His Majesty's permission to speak?"

"You have," said the fat man on the throne. "Rise."

"I greet Your Majesty and humble myself—"

The king held up a pudgy hand. "We'll consider the rest as said, good Master Gezun. We have some questions. First, you look like a Pusâdian, with your stature and curly hair; yet you came to Torrutseish from the east. How is that?"

"I am a Lorska by birth," said Gezun, "but I have wandered far from my homeland. I dislike to expand on my personal affairs, lest Your Majesty find my tale tiresome—"

"Go ahead and expand," said the king. "We are fain to learn of other realms. You were born in windy Lorsk, you say?"

"Aye, sire; on the Bay of Kort, on the western coast of bison-swarming Lorsk, in the seagirt land of Pusâd. I was Döpueng Shysh, the son of a squire, but was stolen by Aremorian pirates whilst still a boy."

Gezun bore a slave brand, faint but still visible, on one hand.

19

Therefore he had given up trying to hide the fact that he had once been a slave, although he knew that to many such a status left an ineradicable stigma of inferiority. He continued:

"I served for years as apprentice to Sancheth Sar, a wizard of Gadaira. Being unable to pronounce my natal name, he called me 'Gezun,' a common servile nomen in those parts; and that is now I have sometimes called myself Gezun of Gadaira.

"At last Sancheth died, having named me his heir, and I set out upon my wanderings—"

"Have you been to Torrutseish before?"

"Aye, sire; eighteen years ago, in the reign of King Ikusiven, in whose menagerie I served for a time as assistant beastkeeper—"

"And whence arrived you this time? From Phaiaxia?"

"Nay, sire. I came by the more northerly route, through Ausonia."

"Tell us of Ausonia," said the king, scratching a flea bite. "Have they still that curious form of governance they call a republic?"

"Aye. They have a Senate and an Assembly; but the rich, who compose the Senate, dominate the public business. . . ."

For an hour Gezun continued to answer the king's questions. This king, he thought, at least seemed to have better sense than some of the royal nonentities and nitwits whom he had met. At last he broke into the flow of geographical questions and answers to say:

"May it please Your Majesty, I should like to lay before you a proposal to increase the wealth of your realm and of your royal treasury. . . ."

Then Gezun gave his prepared address. He told of the Carpet of Khazi and its wondrous powers, glossing over the irregularities of his obtaining it. He set forth his plan for establishing a factory in Torrutseish to make duplicates of this carpet.

"Hold!" said the king. "Not certain are we that your proposal would be to the kingdom's best advantage, Master Gezun. Have you thought of the military applications of this discovery?"

"Well—ah—to tell the truth, sire, I had not. I am a peace-loving fellow."

"Do but stop and think, then. One man, mounted on one of your flying carpets, were worth a whole troop of horse for scouting. Ensconced on such rugs, archers could pour their shafts down upon their foes with virtual impunity. They need but stay above the height to which an upshot arrow can attain.

"In sooth, Master Gezun, we see your project as one conducted in secret, within our very palace, with utmost care to keep the method of ensorcelment from leaking out. Thus should our realm be secured against all foes. Ha! I can see the next band of wild Galathan savages, who shall have crossed our borders to raid our peaceful counties, fleeing in abject terror before a squadron of your flying rugs."

"If Your Majesty please, methinks we could still sell carpets for peaceful purposes also. Buyers could be taught to control the carpets without knowing the spells whereby I imprison the demons in them in the first place."

"Hm, hm," said the king, toying with his beard. "Perhaps you are right. We shall see. In any event, let not this change of plan cark you. If your scheme work, you shall be suitably rewarded.

"Ere we commit ourselves to such a venture, howsomever, we needs must be surer of our footing. Where is this wondrous carpet the now?"

"I brought it to the palace, sire. 'Tis yonder, with my son."

"Then let us see it."

In the courtyard Zhanes dropped the rolled-up rug from his shoulder and spread it on the flagstones. King Norskezhek puffed his way out between the columns that upheld the portico of his hall of audience. With some slight difficulty—for his girth made it hard to bend over—he examined the rug. He asked:

"Where is the demon said to be woven into the fabric?"

Gezun pointed. "Those spots are his eyes, that line of foliage is his head, these patterns make his arms, and so on."

The king squinted through half-closed lids. "We see now. When one looks at the carpet in a certain way, the pattern does make a form like that of a human figure. Is it ready to fly?"

"Aye, sire. Would you have a demonstration?"

"Certes, if you can do it safely. I would not have your brains dashed out by an excess of zeal."

Gezun settled himself cross-legged on the center of the rug and cried, in the secret tongue of the Seteshan wizards: *"Ehara, Yiqqal! Alluba!"*

The carpet shuddered; a rippling motion ran along its fringes. Foot by foot, it rose from the pavement, until it was above the heads of those standing in the courtyard. The carpet continued to rise until it towered above the roof of the palace. Those below burst into cries of wonder. Gezun called:

"Yiqqal! Adoranto, ken duspathwé!"

The rug moved slowly forward, clearing the portico by a good ten feet.

"Biorbo a ra doloja!"

The rug circled to the right, passing over the wall around the royal inclosure and over some of the streets of Torrutseish. Gezun had almost repassed the wall when a child below saw him and screamed. For an instant there was a stir among the common folk in that section. Then the rug passed into the royal inclosure again, and the wall hid the streets from sight. Gezun arrived once more above the palace courtyard.

"Abahé!"

The rug settled gently to the flagstones. The king seized Gezun's hand and hauled him to his feet.

"That was splendid!" said King Norskezhek, beaming through his fat. "I should never have believed it. Can you take me for a ride?"

Gezun was not sure how much weight the demon Yiqqal could support, but he feared to disappoint the king in the latter's enthusiastic mood. He said:

"I'm sure of it, Your Majesty. If you will sit to the rear of the place I occupied, I will take the front—"

22

"Your Majesty!" cried the usher. "That were a violation of all the laws of royal courtesy, to have this low-caste foreigner sit before you!"

"Oh?" said the king.

"Aye, sire. The laws and customs of Tartessia require that you occupy the front seat of any vehicle."

The king looked at Gezun and spread his hands in a helpless gesture. "I am sorry, my friend; but we do have certain rules, and I must set an example."

When the king took the front place on the rug, Gezun found that, seated behind the massive monarch, he could not see where he was going. He moved a little to the left.

"Well, sir?" said the king.

"I fear the balance will be thrown off," said Gezun. "Besides which, Your Majesty is—ah—a trifle larger than I . . ."

"No remarks about my size, Master Gezun, if you please. But I see your point. I suppose one balances this thing much as one would a small boat?"

"Aye, sire."

"Well then—ho, Master Bokarri! You are just the man we need. Seat yourself on the right after corner of the carpet, to balance Master Gezun's weight."

A spasm of terror passed over Bokarri's features, but he gingerly approached the rug. "Here, Your M-majesty?"

"Aye, that should do. Boot, saddle, to horse, and away, Master Gezun!"

"*Alluba!*" cried Gezun.

Like a living thing, the rug stirred, fluttered, and crawled beneath the weight of the three men. At last it began to rise, but so slowly that its motion could hardly be perceived. Moreover, since King Norskezhek weighed more than Gezun and Bokarri combined, the rug developed a notable slope, down in front and up in the rear. As they rose to the level of the pediment over the colonnade, the carpet began to move forward without any command from Gezun,

23

who nonetheless had some idea of what was happening. Yiqqal was in the position of a man supporting a badly balanced tray, who moves in the direction the tray is tipping in a frantic effort to keep it from spilling its contents.

Bokarri screamed as the roof ornaments above the pediment swooped at them. There was a slight jar as the rug touched the head of the royal stone owl that sat on the end of the ridgepole. Teetering wildly, the rug sailed on. Bokarri threw himself down on his face and clung to the edges of the carpet.

"Lie back, King! Lie back!" shouted Gezun.

Pale under his swarthiness, King Norskezhek glanced back at Gezun and obeyed.

Thus relieved of the unbalance, the rug steadied. Gezun called for a right turn and brought the vehicle back over the courtyard. Then, before Gezun could command the descent, the rug tilted again and began to spin round and round.

"Hold on!" shouted Gezun as the carpet spun faster and faster, slowly descending like a falling autumn leaf.

The façades surrounding the courtyard fled past Gezun's vision in a blur. He cried: *"Pala! Pala! Dohaso! Afwanthaso!"* But the rug continued to gyrate until it settled with a bump and a scrape on the flagstones.

Staggering with dizziness, the king heaved himself up. Although still pale, he maintained his royal dignity.

"Good Master Gezun," he said, "methinks you need a bit more practice in governing your celestial steed ere you take passengers aloft. How fares Master Bokarri?"

Bokarri had fainted. A little water in the face and a swallow of wine revived him.

"Ten thousand pardons, Your Majesty!" quoth Gezun. "'Twas utter stupidity on my part so to overload my poor demon. Next time—"

"There shall be no next time so far as I am concerned," said the king. "Once was more than enow."

24

"But, sire! Think of the possibilities! You would not deprive the Tartessian Empire of this device merely because of a blunder on my part, now would you?"

King Norskezhek stared silently at Gezun, then replied, "There may be somewhat in that, my good man. Take your magical carpet away, study the science of constructing them some more, practice control of these things in the air, and ask my secretary for another audience—let's say—a moon from today. This has been a memorable adventure, albeit more amusing in retrospect than at the time. Fare you well!"

The king waddled back into his palace, followed by his crowd of servants and courtiers. This left Gezun, Bokarri, and Zhanes alone in the courtyard, save for the ever-present guards.

Gezun rolled up the rug, placed it across his shoulder, and started for the vestibule. Bokarri followed, grumbling:

"You idiot, to have taken up the king before you had fully practiced! Would you set a riding novice on a ferocious war stallion?"

"'Twas not that. The king asked for a ride, and I saw no good way to refuse him. He's touchy about his fat, and I overestimated Yiqqal's capacity. Belike the demon could have borne the king alone, but the three of us were too much. On the other hand, I had to go along to command Yiqqal."

"What will you do now?"

They passed out the main gate to the palace grounds. Gezun said:

"Follow the king's command, I suppose. But I shall have to find gainful employment. My trade metal will not last a month in this costly city."

"Think not to sponge off me!" snarled Bokarri. "If you're pressed for means, sell your horses and trap."

"Who spoke of sponging? All I'll ask of you is to put me in the way of a little magical trade—horoscopes, prophetic trances, simple sorceries, and the like. As president of the guild, you can do that."

"You would have to join our guild; and, being a foreigner, you would find that this took time. Of course, could you present a sumptuous gift to our brotherhood, things might be speeded . . ."

"Sumptuous gifts I have none, save this carpet on my shoulder. Did I present that to the guild, the profits were divided amongst all the members. How many have you?"

"Forty-six masters, together with a hundred-odd apprentices, who vote not and would not share in such a distribution."

"Very well! Which would you prefer: a third of the profits or one part in forty-six?"

"I shall have to think this over," mumbled Bokarri. "You nearly ended my poor old life from sheer terror today, and I'm dubious about joining my fortunes to such a scatterwit."

"Am I the only sorcerer whose works ever went awry?" said Gezun. "Meseems you've suffered reverses in your time, too."

Bokarri grunted.

"Think, then," continued Gezun. "Put no obstacles in the way of my gaining a livelihood, and a month from today we shall return to the king."

5

IN A LOCKED chamber of the Guildhall, the president of the carters' guild addressed the heads of the guilds of horse copers, porters, horsecoursers, grooms, knackers, chairmen, farriers, muleteers, assmen, wainwrights, coachmen, boatmen, and messengers, who sat about a long table with drinking jacks of barley beer and perry before them. He said:

"You have all, I am sure, heard the rumors wherewith the town has buzzed for the last two days, of the flying carpet of Master Gezun of Lorsk."

"I've heard little else," said the chief of the knackers, who made saddles and harness. "I believe it not, though. The mob is ever exciting itself with tales of bleeding statues, talking oxen, and the descent of some god to earth. This, meseems, is but another tittle-tattle of the same sort."

"Master Naskanin," said the carter, "wouldst take me for a credulous man?"

"Nay, good Master Ezvelar," said the knacker. "Forsooth, you've always borne yourself as a man of sound common sense."

"Would you say I was given to delusions or wild fancies?"

"Nor that, either."

"Well then, I saw this soaring rug with mine own eyes, and they are good eyes for one of my ripe years."

"Good my sir!" exclaimed the knacker.

"Aye. I was driving my cart along King Asizhen Street, where it adjoins the wall of the palace grounds, when the cry of a child caused me to pull up. The tot was pointing skyward. Following her gesture, I saw the rug, with a single man upon it, vanish over the palace wall.

"Others, too, had seen; and for some time there was a stirring and a running and a chattering, like unto the scurrying of ants when their nest be disturbed. Things had just begun to quiet down, and the folk to go about their business, when the thing swooped over the wall again. This time it bore two or three persons; 'twas hard to see, for they were crouched down on the upper surface. It seemed to labor and wobble through the air, as if the force upholding it were too weak for the task. Methought 'twould crash into the wall in its course; but it cleared the obstacle by the breadth of a hair and vanished again.

"For a time I was too mazed to do more than gaup. But then I bethought me of my duties to my guild. My researches brought me at last to one of our members, hight Barik, who drives the dung cart for the palace. At my behest Barik inquired among the palace people and gathered enough stories to have a good picture of what had befallen.

"This Gezun of Lorsk appeared half a moon ago out of the east, bringing this ensorcelled carpet with him. He went into partnership with Bokarri, the chief of the wizards' guild, to exploit the invention. They say today's show went not altogether well, what of our noble king's port and the unskill of this strange craft's pilot."

"I heard that too," said the chief muleteer. "I also heard that the king, in a rage, ordered Master Gezun's instant execution. Some say by beheading, some by burning, and some by impalement; but I doubt not that the deed's been done."

"Your sources are garbled, more's the pity," said the carter. "Gezun's alive and well in his quarters, selling love potions, finding lost bangles, and raising the ghosts of dear departeds. But within the next moon he'll be back at court, beguiling the king with tales of the virtues of his device. The king was overheard inviting him."

"So what?" said the chief messenger. "If Master Gezun be fain to risk his neck on this contraption, that's his affair. Why call us hither to discuss it?"

"There's much more to it than a simple risking of necks. Gezun plans to multiply this thing and sell it to all and sundry."

"Well?" said the messenger.

"See you not, Master Tiaush? If the carpets multiply, what will befall your livelihood and mine? They'll be clean ruined, that's what! So will yours, and yours, and yours . . ." He went around the circle, pointing at each of the guild presidents in turn until he came to the end.

The guild chiefs looked at one another uneasily. The president of the chairmen said, "By Aphradexa's teats, I begin to see. What rich man would hire a pair of lusty chairmen to lug his sedan across the city, when he has but to sit on his rug, say 'hocus pocus,' and presto! he's at his goal in three winks!"

"And who," said the horse coper, "will bother with a horse, to be jounced and bounced and perhaps thrown off and trampled or bitten, when he can glide aloft on the air, like a boat on the sea?"

"And if there be no horses, there'll be no call for shoeing 'em," said the farrier.

"And merchants will ferry their goods on flying rugs, 'stead of on the backs of mules and asses," said the assman.

"In other words," said the porter, "this dirty foreigner and his devilish device threaten us all with starvation. But what's to do? Hire a bravo to murther him?"

"I have already looked into that matter," said the carter. "Some of my acquaintances are not of the most respectable, and through them I have sent a discreet inquiry into the underworld. The answer is: Not on your life. Some wouldn't mind cutting a throat, but not the throat of a man in favor with the king."

"His favor is not so solid as all that," said the farrier. "He all but slew the king with his tricks."

"Natheless," said the carter, "the king has decided to give him another chance, and Norskezhek the Stout is no man to brook the slaying of one whom he has bidden to his court. He'd turn Torrutseish upside down to find the slayer."

"What, then?" asked the porter. "Hire a witch-wife to burke him by invultuation, with a waxen image and pins?"

"Nay; they're all under the presidency of Bokarri, who is hand in glove with Gezun."

"Wait a bit," said the chairman. "Meseems I now recall some events of nigh twenty years agone, wherein Masters Gezun and Bokarri figured. There was some quarrel over a Hesperian wench and over some magical bauble. It fell to my lot to bear the litter of Lord Noish to his doom in the tower of Zyc the Hercynian. In the course of this journey we were set upon by a band of rogues led by this same Gezun. They were driven off; but later the same night, I heard, Gezun quarreled with Bokarri—who was also entwined in this coil—over that magical thingummy. Gezun felled Bokarri with a mighty blow and fled with the instrument, leaving Bokarri swearing eternal vengeance."

"It does not look like eternal vengeance now," said the messenger.

"I've known Bokarri for many years," said the carter. "Take it from me, he's no man to forget a grudge. If he seems to go along with Gezun now, 'tis either that he bides his time to entrap Gezun anon, or else his avarice—a quality as well developed as his rancor—has overcome his lust for vengeance."

"Well, then," said the boatman, who had kept silence up to now, "if rancor and avarice pull in contrary directions in Bokarri's breast, let's make it so that they pull together. The results will be that much more probable, even as the tides of the Western Ocean be greater when the sun and moon pull together than when they be in quartile."

"What mean you, Master Vennok?"

"Methinks there's enough in the treasuries of our respective guilds to offer Bokarri a larger sum for disposing of Master Gezun than he's likely to gain from Gezun's fantastic scheme. If any man can do it without leaving a trace—or rather, leaving traces pointing in wrong directions—'tis that old he-witch!"

The other presidents spoke in turn, all applauding the boatman's recommendation.

"Then we're agreed," said Ezvelar the carter. "Let me caution you to say nought till the deed's done, lest the weavers' guild get wind of it. Thinking to profit from Gezun's scheme, they might well oppose us.

"Now comes the hard part. 'Tis easy to cheer the plan but not so easy to decide how much to assess each guild. Order more perry and beer, Jutenas. This bids fair to be a lengthy chaffer."

As the festival of Dzerevan, the king of the gods, approached, Bokarri the wizard shut himself in his cabinet and commanded his apprentices to leave him severely alone, for he had a mighty magical work to accomplish. On his workbench he spread out his magical paraphernalia and two small objects. One was a patch of uncured hide, an inch square, covered with coarse black animal hair. The other was a pinch of human hair, glossy black with a few gray hairs. It was, in fact, the hair of Gezun of Lorsk, obtained by bribery from the barber who had lately given Gezun a trim.

6

GEZUN'S SECOND audience with King Norskezhek was set for noon on the day of the feast of Dzerevan. Ordinarily the king would not have granted any audiences on that day. The day was supposed to be devoted to religious rituals, the final bullfight of the season, and a grand feast and revel in the evening.

Lately, however, there had been a rush of royal business: pirates of the Gorgon Isles threatening the port of Gadaira at the mouth of the Baitis, a dispute with the king of Aremoria, and bickering with the Galathan tribes to the northeast. Gezun therefore found his audience squeezed in between the rites of Dzerevan in the morning and the bullfight in the afternoon.

The day before Zhanes and Ugaph had expressed the wish to attend the bullfight. Gezun squelched this.

"If your mother is fain to take you—"

"I am not," said Ro.

"Then you'll have to do without. I cannot possibly give the king his demonstration and then dash off home to fetch you to this gory spectacle. I'll tell you: I promise soon to take you fishing on the Baitis."

At the time for the audience, Gezun was kept waiting. The king appeared, puffing and sweating and gnawing the leg of a fowl. He cut Gezun's courtesies short.

"All right," he said, "show us your piloting. Make it not too long, or we shall be late for the tauromachy."

Gezun seated himself on the Carpet of Khazi and commanded Yiqqal. The demonstration went off without a hitch. Gezun soared and swooped and performed tight circles before alighting on the flagstones.

"Good!" said the king. "We have decided to back your project. The usher will present you with a letter of credit on the royal treasury for five hundred nasses of gold. This will enable you to set up your factory. Order no new buildings nor any other unneeded extravagance; there are plenty of suitable quarters for rent in Torrutseish. See our secretary for another meeting to settle details. And now you must excuse us; we are off to preside at the bullfight. Fare you well!"

Gezun began, "I earnestly thank Your Majesty—" when something strange happened. He stared wildly, staggered, and fell to all fours. He opened his mouth as if to speak, but only an inarticulate cry, like the moo of a cow, came forth.

"Good gods!" exclaimed the king. "The poor fellow has gone mad. You men, seize him ere he hurt himself. Find where he dwells, carry him thither, and deliver him to the care of his family. And now we're off."

As his consciousness cleared, Gezun realized that he was in a stall or inclosure and that something strange had happened to his vision. He then observed that he was on all fours. He tried to stand up, but this proved unexpectedly difficult, as if either his legs had weakened or his weight had increased. He opened his mouth to cry, "What in the nine hells is this?"

But only a bellow came forth. He swung his head to see better, and something attached to his head came into jarring contact with a wooden wall. He looked down at his hands and saw a pair of black-furred legs ending in cloven hooves.

Then Gezun knew what had happened. His soul had been transferred by magic to the body of a bull. Presumably the bull's soul had been put into his own body.

Cautiously he explored his prison. There was a pile of hay at the end he faced, and a rope around his horns limited his movement.

He braced himself and reared, planting his fore hooves on the top of the partition, and looked over a row of similar stalls. In some of these stalls he could see, over the barriers, the tips of the horns of more aurochs bulls. At the end of the passage on which these stalls faced, the bright noon spring sun flooded the opening. Beyond Gezun glimpsed the sand of the arena.

The world looked strangely different to his bull's vision. It was a colorless world of blacks, whites, and grays. Moreover, since both his eyes no longer focused on the same objective, it was a flat world, without depth. On the other hand, it was a world of much keener smells.

There was a sore spot on his back, as of a small, superficial wound not completely healed. Flies buzzed around it, bothering him.

Evidently, Gezun thought, he was in the body of one of the bulls to be slain at the final tauromachy of the season. The stalls were under the spectators' benches. From his position nearest the open end of the passage he suspected that he would be the first to be sent into the ring.

Who, he wondered, had done this to him, and why? With whom had he dealt in Torrutseish? The king, certainly; but it was absurd to think that the king would get rid of him in so elaborate a way when he had merely to say, "Off with his head!"

Furthermore, Gezun knew that only a very powerful spell could effect this transposition of souls. It would take long and costly preparations. It required a sample of organic matter from the two living beings to be manipulated. (Was that the reason for the sore on his back?) It left the thaumaturge exhausted for days. And, like most spells that modified the natural state of things, its effect was only temporary.

If Gezun could stay alive for a few hours or days, his soul would return to its proper body—if that body had not been destroyed in the meantime. Likewise the bull's soul would return to its own body, if that body had not perished in the arena. If the bull's body were slain while Gezun's soul occupied it, Gezun would be dead.

Who, then, would have the magical skill for this? Bokarri was an obvious suspect. Having presented Gezun at court as he had promised, he was no longer bound by the oath he had sworn on his magical powers. Bokarri had never been a very able wizard when Gezun had known him before, but he might have improved in eighteen years.

Why, however, should Bokarri wish to do Gezun in? There was the old grudge over Gezun's taking the ring. But Bokarri had seemed to accept Gezun's offer of restitution, by making Bokarri a partner in the flying-carpet business.

Had Bokarri been feigning all along, awaiting a chance for revenge? Had he wished to destroy Gezun at the start, surely there were quicker and easier methods. He could, for instance, have rounded up a few cronies in the magicians' guild and performed a simultaneous invultuation on Gezun. The victim might have stood off one such attack but would likely have succumbed to those from several foes at once.

No, there was more to this than met the eye. There must be some other factor that had arrayed a powerful magician—perhaps Bokarri, perhaps another—against him.

Time might discover the mystery. Meanwhile, Gezun's task was to stay alive until the effects of the soul transferrence wore off. He absently munched hay while running over what he knew of Tartessian tauromachy and the Tartessians' attitudes toward it.

During the next hour the murmur of the crowd increased as spectators straggled into the bull ring and found their seats. Gezun ate hay (which he found surprisingly tasty to his bull's tongue) and planned his future actions.

At last the trumpet blew and the band struck up. Over the wall of his pen Gezun glimpsed a throng of gaily costumed bullfighters debouching from a side passage into the corridor on which the bull pens fronted and marching out into the arena.

Then he heard and smelled other men moving around the outside of his pen. A sharp pain in his back made him start and jerk about, until he realized that a handler had reached over the top of the pen and thrust the bronzen pin with the colored ribbons into his back.

For a moment the bull part of Gezun's nature took over. Rage crowded out thought; all he could think of was the pleasure of catching one of these two-legged monkeys and goring and trampling it into a shapeless, bloody mush. Then, as the gate before him swung open, his human intelligence fought its way back into control.

He stepped out into the passage. The open gate blocked off the way to the outside, leaving open only the path to the arena. He cantered out into the sand and the glare, as he had seen other bulls do. His movements were clumsy at first but became smoother as he caught the knack of handling his bovine body.

Four chulos stood about the ring, holding the cloaks wherewith they hoped to lure him into futile, exhausting charges. Ignoring the chulos, Gezun trotted across the arena and stood in front of the royal box. He formally bowed to the king and dropped to one knee.

A murmur of amazement ran through the crowd, which filled every seat in the structure. Gezun rose to his four feet again. Two chulos approached him, waving their cloaks. Instead of charging them, he lay down, rolled over on his back, and waved his hooves in the air. He made several rolls in succession before rising to his feet again.

From the audience came an outburst of cries: some of laughter, some of indignation. Gezun guessed that among those who took their bullfighting seriously, many would be outraged by his performance.

Now he faced a chulo with a cloak. Instead of charging the cloak, he swerved at the last instant so as to butt the chulo in the midriff.

35

Gezun took care that one horn went to each side of the man, so that he was not gored, merely hurled to the sand. Two other chulos rushed out to divert Gezun by waving their cloaks. He ignored them and watched the fallen man. When the latter got to his feet, Gezun lunged again and butted him to the ground.

After the third fall the man scrambled up and ran away, leaving his cloak. Gezun caught the cloak on the point of one horn, walked before the king's box, and gravely laid the cloak in the sand in front of the king.

The noise in the audience grew louder. Gezun could catch only an occasional word, but there seemed to be a lot of quarreling and shouting between those who laughed at Gezun's antics and those enraged by them.

Gezun turned to the nearest chulo, who stood nervously flapping his cloak. He knocked the man down, placed a fore hoof on his stomach, and licked his face with a huge red tongue.

The shouting now had spread to the official personnel of the bull ring, who were stationed on the ground between the inner and outer barriers.

Gezun turned over the man he was holding down, slid the point of one horn under the back of the man's jacket, and with a wrench tore the garment loose from its wearer. With the wreck of the jacket dangling from his horn, he again walked over to the royal box and laid the rag on top of the cloak.

A glance up showed Gezun that fist fights had broken out among the audience. Some shouted, "Hurrah for the bull! Let him live!" while others screamed, "Futter the bull! He is possessed of a demon! Slay him, lest he dishonor our noble sport forever!"

Gezun feinted a charge toward the nearest chulos, who dodged back through the openings in the inner barrier. None seemed eager to try conclusions with so unpredictable a beast.

Instead a darter on foot came out the gate and started for Gezun with his darts held high. Gezun had studied the approach used by darters: the dancing step to the side just as the bull began his charge.

Gezun began his charge according to the program. Then, just as the darter extended himself to plant his darts, Gezun whirled to present his rump to the man and lashed out with both hind feet. The hooves caught the bullfighter in the midriff and hurled him several paces away.

Gezun turned back and bounded to where his victim lay. Ignoring the frantic efforts of the chulos to divert him, he examined the man. Having had the wind knocked out of him, the darter was coughing and gasping for breath. Gezun hooked a horn under the belt that upheld the man's breeches. He bore him to the barrier and, with a jerk of his head, hurled the darter clear over. Then he turned and started for the king's box again, executing a little dance step on the way.

Uproar and fighting had spread all over the stands. King Norskezhek was on his feet, shouting commands. A motley group of armed men issued from the main gate. Some were royal guards, some regular soldiers, and some bullfighters armed with bull-killing lances. An officer yelled at them to get into formation. A couple of slingers in this troop wound up and let fly at Gezun. One missed, and the other's leaden bullet glanced off Gezun's leathery hide.

A pair of Tartessians, locked in combat, rolled down a flight of steps and over the outer barrier. A man with a knife chased another man along one of the upper benches, screaming epithets. Members of the civic guard whacked at rioters with their staves.

The armed men in the arena hesitantly approached Gezun. Since they were between him and the only escape route, he gave a sudden bellow and charged them. They scattered, and he burst through their line. A sting told him that one of their spears had wounded him in the side. Then he found the gate closed.

He poked at the gate with a horn, but it would not open. Then he saw why. It was closed by a simple bolt. This bolt had a pair of handles, one on the outer side and one, projecting through a slot in the wood, on the inner side where Gezun stood. He placed the tip of a horn against the bolt handle and pushed the bolt back.

Another sting, this time in the rump, told him that his foes were upon him again. He whirled to face them. They stood in a crescent formation; one had poked him with a lance. Behind them Gezun sighted King Norskezhek. The king, realizing that his officer was not making headway with his detachment, had descended into the arena to take command himself.

With his loudest bellow Gezun charged the line again. The man scrambled out of his way, and he bore down on the king. Norskezhek turned to run but tripped on his spangled robe and fell sprawling. His crown came off and rolled across the sand like a small golden hoop.

Gezun bounded over the king's bulky form and caught the crown on the point of one horn. He circled around to return to the gate, while men leaped out of his path. At the gate he found the bolt still drawn back. He hooked a horn into the jamb, pried the gate open, and galloped through.

Minutes later the guards at the east gate of Torrutseish were astonished to see a huge black aurochs, with a golden crown spiked on one horn, thunder up to the gate and through. One guard witlessly began his formula, "Halt! State your name, nation, and business—" but the bull was through before he had gotten out half the words.

7

Gezun arrived at his house and tried to enter, forgetting that he was much too large. He managed to get his muzzle in the front door. While his wife and children cowered away from this apparition, he cried, "Ro, darling!"

But it only came out as a bellow. Then a dizziness seized him.

He staggered—and found himself back in his human form, but tied hand and foot under some dark substance that pressed down upon him. It was stuffy and dusty.

"Ho!" he shouted. "Where am I?"

Ro and the children rushed into the bedroom and pulled Gezun out from under the bed. Ro asked:

"Are you really, truly yourself again?"

"Of course I'm myself! Who thought you I was?"

"What is your name?"

"Gezun of Lorsk, born Döpueng Shysh. Bokarri transposed my soul with that of an aurochs destined to be slain in the bull ring today, but now the spell has worn off."

"Was that you who thrust its great black head in the door just now, frightening us to death?" Ro worked at the knots of the cords that bound him.

"Aye. What became of the beast?"

"It clattered off down the street. Then I heard you call—"

"What's befallen here since Bokarri's spell took effect? I was at the palace, getting a document from the king, when I found myself in the bull's body."

"Some men from the palace brought you here, bound hand and foot. Since you were plainly out of your mind, I put you to bed, leaving you tied. Then a band of rough-looking men burst in with cudgels, demanding the Carpet of Khazi and you—"

"You didn't give them the carpet?" cried Gezun.

"What else could I do? It was there in plain sight. I pretended not to understand Euskerian and told the children in my own tongue to hide you whilst I slew time with these invaders."

"Who were they, have you any idea?"

"I recognized one: the porter who helped us to move our new furniture in, and I think another was one of the grooms at the stable where we keep our equipage."

"How did you hide me?"

"The children found you too heavy to lift from the bed, but at

39

last they tipped you off the edge and pulled the bed over you."

"What did the gang?"

"Not seeing you beneath the bed, they bore off the rug. One said —as nearly as I could understand his Euskerian—something like: 'Ruin our livelihood and reduce us to starvation, would he?' And another muttered: 'The rascal's gotten clean away, but at least we can destroy his damnable rug.' And another: 'The old witch-man failed us, but the gods help those who help themselves.' The next thing that happened was that the bull thrust its head in the door."

"Aha!" said Gezun. "So the guilds were after me lest I minish their employment? Flog me, but I should have thought of that! And they doubtless hired old Bokarri to switch souls on me. Darling, if our stable boys are in on the plot, belike 'twere wiser not to show my face there. Could you command them to hitch up the team, and then could you drive it around to our door whilst I pack our gear?"

Gezun's carriage rocketed north under a gibbous moon. A lion roared in the distance. Ro said:

"Whither are we going?"

"To Kerys, the capital of Aremoria," said Gezun.

"Have you any old foes there?"

"I've never even been in Kerys, so it is unlikely that I should have enemies there."

"Perhaps not; but still, with your talent for making them—"

"Besides, since Aremorian pirates kidnapped and enslaved me as a boy, the Aremorians owe me something."

"How will you make a living?" asked Ro.

"I still know the secret of flying carpets. Had Bokarri's gang slain me, there had been no man west of Kheru with this knowledge. As it is, I need not the carpet itself; I can make my own."

"Think you to beguile the king of Aremoria into backing you, as you did Norskezhek?"

"That wants thinking on. A more circumspect approach is indicated."

"And whilst you scheme and maneuver, what shall the children and I eat?"

Gezun chuckled. "Ugaph, reach me that bundle of sacking atop the cedar chest. Nay, the other one."

Driving with one hand, Gezun unwrapped the bundle with the other and held up King Norskezhek's crown. "I fled from the arena with this thing dangling from one of my horns. When I came nigh unto our house, I tossed it on a rubbish heap in an alley. After I had regained my true shape, and whilst you were fetching the carriage, I ran out and found the gewgaw; no passerby had marked it.

"It should keep us in comfort for some time, if I'm careful in disposing of it. Should I pry out the gems and melt up the gold? That were safer but would bring a smaller return. On t'other hand, the thing has sentimental value for the Tartessians, who would pay more than its nominal value for its return; but they might also lay me by the heels. . . ."

Ro sighed. "Dear, silly Gezun! You may not be the world's best man, but at least life with you is surely never tedious."

Mnera said, "What Mommy really means is that she's getting a little old to catch another man, so she needs must make the best of the one she has."

"Hush, girl!" said Gezun. "Such worldly cynicism is unseemly in one so young. Kiss me, everybody, and ho for Kerys!"

Most Sword & Sorcery heroes tend to be little more than slight variations on the model of Conan—strong-jawed Barbarian warrior heroes with burning eyes, bulging thews and burnished broadswords. Not so with Elric.

Elric of Melniboné is the creation of a marvelously gifted young British writer named Michael Moorcock. Born, I believe, in 1939, Moorcock is now—at thirty-two—the youngest member of SAGA. He is also one of the most widely published of us all, for he has been writing and selling stories ever since he was a boy of fifteen. In all that time Moorcock has done a little of everything, from the formal science fiction of *The Ice Schooner* and *The Fireclown* to the heroic fantasy of *The Eternal Champion* and his Dorian Hawkmoon tetralogy. He has also tried his hand at the ever-popular field of Burroughsian pastiche with three excellent novels of Martian adventure, first published under the pseudonym of Edward P. Bradbury and now reappearing at the time of this writing with new titles but under his own name. As if that were not enough, Mike Moorcock has edited a couple of handfuls of science fiction anthologies, is the editor of the famous British magazine *New Worlds*, and has published eight or nine novels so recently, and so rapidly, that I cannot keep up with reading him and have fallen far behind.

It just shows how much you can get done when you start selling at fifteen and devote half your lifetime to writing!

Out of all this plethora of books and sequels and trilogies and stuff, Moorcock's most lasting work remains his tales of Elric of

Melniboné. No brawny barbarian, Elric is a sickly albino princeling of a dead empire. No stalwart hero, Elric is in fact a doomed and tragic figure—the villain of his own grim epic.

Chained in symbiotic servitude to his enchanted sword, Stormbringer, which vampirically feeds on the life-force of those it slays, accompanied by his own Sancho Panza, the enigmatic little Moonglum, Elric wanders homelessly over the surface of his lost world in search of the peace he can never really find. . . .

THE first Elric stories were collected in book form under the title of *The Stealer of Souls* (London, 1963), published when their author was only twenty-four. In 1965 followed an Elric novel called *Stormbringer,* wherein Moorcock made the tactical error of killing off his hero and terminating the series by the simple method of blowing up the universe. Since then Mike has created many another fantasy hero, but he has recently confessed to me that he is tired of making up carbon copies of Elric: hence this story, and the good news that he is back at work, fitting new Elric tales in among the ones written almost a decade earlier.

For those readers who like to follow the internal sequence of a story series, this tale belongs between "The Singing Citadel" and "The Stealer of Souls." Moorcock wrote me about his new Elrics: "I decided that rather than try to invent another character like him, I might just as well keep writing about him."

A splendid idea! And Mike's hand has not lost its touch, as the following story demonstrates.

The Jade Man's Eyes

by MICHAEL MOORCOCK

INTRODUCTION

For ten thousand years did the Bright Empire of Melniboné rule the world by virtue of her Sorcerer Kings, her Dragon Hordes and her golden battle-barges. From Imrryr, the Dreaming City, capital of the Isle of Melniboné, the power of the Bright Emperors radiated over all the lands of mankind, though the Melnibonéans were not true men themselves. They were tall, with eldritch features. They were proud, malicious, sensitive and artistic, with a vast knowledge of sorcery. They were familiar with many of the supernatural Realms of the Higher Worlds and knew that the wonders of Earth could not compare with those of those Higher Worlds. They regarded their late-born cousins of the Young Kingdoms with arrogant contempt, reckoning them fit only to be plundered or enslaved.

But at last, after a hundred centuries, Melniboné's power began to wane as she was shaken by the casting of frightful runes, attacked by powers even greater than she, until all that was left of the Bright Empire was the Isle itself and its single city, Imrryr, still strong, still feared, still the mercantile capital of the world, but no longer the glorious power she had been.

And so it might have remained, save that it was not Destiny's way to have it so.

For the next few centuries, which was called the Age of the Young Kingdoms, petty empires rose and fell and new nations had their moments of power—Sheegoth, Maidahk, S'aaleem, Ilmiora and others. And then came a great movement upon the Earth and above it: the destiny of Men and Gods was hammered out upon the forge of Fate and monstrous wars were brewed and mighty deeds performed. And during this time there rose up many heroes.

Chief of these was Elric, last ruler of Melniboné, who bore the rune-carved Black Sword, Stormbringer.

Hero, perhaps, is not the proper term for Elric, for it was he who turned against his own line and led the Sea Lords of the Young Kingdoms in their mighty attack upon Imrryr—an attack which resulted in Imrryr's destruction and theirs. But it was all part of Fate's plan, though Elric was not to learn this for many years.

Elric of Melniboné, proud prince of ruins, last lord of a dying race, became a wanderer, loathed and feared throughout the lands of the Young Kingdoms. Elric of the Black Sword, sorcerer and slayer of kin, despoiler of his homeland, crimson-eyed albino, who had within him a greater destiny than he knew . . .

. . . Now there was a certain sorcerer of Pan Tang called Theleb K'aarna. Elric, whose vengeful emotions had already brought much grief to himself and others, bore a grudge against the sorcerer and spent three years in pursuit of him until he was at last tracked to Bakshaan, a city rich enough to make all the other cities of the North East seem poor, where, in a melancholy adventure, he was slain at last.

46

. . . Short-statured Moonglum, of the red hair and wide grin, wanted to head southeast for the peaceful lands of Ilmiora, but Elric was drawn back to the Southern Continent, where he spent the winter squandering his treasure in the cities of Argimiliar, seeking an impossible consolation . . .

—The Chronicle of the Black Sword

1

OF ALL THE cities of the Young Kingdoms the city named Chalal was deemed the most beautiful. Some said that it ranked with Imrryr, the Dreaming City of Melniboné, but those who had seen both said that Chalal's beauty was more humane.

Chalal had been built on both banks of the river Cha, which ran through the country of Pikarayd, laid out by a line of artist kings according to the original conception of Mornir the First. Its broad avenues were overlooked by monuments, statues and widely spaced buildings of singularly delicate architecture. White marble, polished granite and alabaster shone in the clear, bright air and there were fine lawns, gardens and evergreens, fountains and mazes, all designed by the greatest artists of the Young Kingdoms through many generations. Chalal was Pikarayd's greatest treasure and for a long while the country had been pauperized to create it.

It happened that one springtime two strange men came to Chalal. They rode their weary Shazarian horses along the quays of marble and lapis lazuli beside the fast-flowing river. One was very tall, with a bone white skin, crimson eyes and hair the color of milk, and he carried a huge, scabbarded broadsword at his side. The other was short, with red hair and a sardonic expression on his face. He bore

47

two swords, one of which was long and curved while its mate was scarcely bigger than a dagger.

Both the men had evidently been traveling for some time, for their clothes were dusty and their features grimed. They might have been unsuccessful merchants or mercenaries who were between wars. But some who saw them enter Chalal recognized the tall man and guessed who his companion was. Those who did recognize the newcomers did not greet their arrival with any pleasure, for Elric of Melniboné was known as a murderer, a traitor and a killer of his own kin who brought horror and destruction wherever he went.

Moonglum of Elwher grinned as they passed a glowering face near one of the many lovely bridges which crossed the Cha.

"I do not think we are welcome here, Elric."

Elric shrugged and gave a half smile. "Who can blame them for not wanting us here to disturb the tranquillity of their city?"

Moonglum grinned through his mask of dust. "Mayhap they're willing to pay us to go elsewhere? Our purses sag like the stomachs of starved cows thanks to your extravagance. Chalal is said to be an expensive city. Every traveler must pay a tax towards the up-keep of all this beauty."

"They'll have trouble obtaining that tax from us. Come, let's cross this bridge and seek a hostelry we can afford."

They turned their horses and began to trot over a bridge of carved granite decorated with statues of Pikarayd's mythological heroes.

They were almost halfway across when Moonglum pointed ahead. A company of horsemen were riding at great speed toward the bridge. They were clad in gilded armor and heavy white cloaks drifted out behind them. Their leader had a full helm with a crest of scarlet plumes. His visor was shut and completely hid his face. Politely Moonglum and Elric drew their own horses aside to let the cavalry pass. The leader acknowledged this action with a salute as he went by and then jerked his helm around to regard Elric, as if in recognition. Then the horsemen had ridden past and continued up a broad avenue between chestnut trees whose leaves had just begun to open.

"That knight must have seen you before," Moonglum said. "By the style of his arms he was not of Chalal. I pray he's not one of those who bears a grudge against you."

"There are many such," Elric said carelessly, "but none has ever managed to satisfy his vengeance."

"They would be fools to try while you bear the Black Sword."

"Aye." Elric sighed and pretended to take an interest in the workmanship of an archway under which they now rode.

They spent the next several hours in searching for an inn, but found none they could afford for even one night. There were no poor quarters in Chalal, no hostelries which catered for those with little money. Their inquiries revealed that the nearest township was a good two days ride away.

Night fell and Moonglum's expression grew increasingly downcast.

"We must find an income, friend Elric," he said. "Could you not magic us a treasure?"

"I have no skill in such conjurings," Elric replied absently.

"Then we must seek employment. Merchants come and go from here. Perhaps they would pay us to protect their caravans. If we went to the quarter where the traders stay we might—"

"Do what you will, Moonglum." Elric dismounted from his horse and led it toward a great marble monument that had been erected upon a lawn of small white flowers. The horse began to crop at the flowers and Elric settled himself with his back at the base of the monument. "I'll sleep here. The night is warm enough." He wrapped his weather-stained cloak about him and closed his eyes.

Moonglum knew that it was impossible to talk to his friend when he sank into one of these moods. He hesitated for a moment and then rode off toward the river.

The night grew colder and Elric awoke shivering from a dark dream. Clouds had covered the moon and it was hard to see more than a few feet in any direction. He got up and stretched his arms. Then he saw the lights. There were about a dozen of them bobbing along the road toward him. He leaned against the monument and watched them with curiosity. He soon saw that the lights were lanterns carried by horsemen dressed in leather caps and jerkins, bearing oval shields, swords and staves. When they saw Elric they dismounted and approached him in a body, opening their lanterns so that light fell upon him.

The leader peered at Elric, whose face was hidden in the cowl of his cloak.

"What do you here, stranger?"

"I was attempting to sleep," Elric replied. "But you and your weather have prevented that between you."

"Why do you not sleep in one of the hostelries yonder?"

"Because I cannot afford their prices," Elric said reasonably.

"Have you paid the Traveler's Tax?"

"I have not."

The leader had a red, belligerent face, and now it frowned deeply. "Then you have broken two of Chalal's few laws already, and doubtless there are others you have broken which we shall yet discover."

"Doubtless. Now be about your business, friend, and I will attempt to continue my sleep."

"You are addressing an official of the Watch," said the man, pursing his lips. "It is my duty to collect the Traveler's Tax and to arrest vagrants who offend the eye of those who come to look upon Chalal's beauty."

"I would advise you to forget your duty in this instance," Elric said softly. "I care nothing for the laws of mankind and these laws of yours seem of even smaller importance than most. Begone!"

"By Valsaq, you're impertinent! I'm a tolerant man. I might even have had mercy on you if you had agreed to leave at once. But now . . ."

Elric pushed back his cloak and put his hand on Stormbringer's hilt. The sword stirred slightly. "I tell you to go," he said grimly. "You will surely die if I draw this blade!"

The captain of the Watch smiled and indicated the dozen men behind him. "Do not be foolish, stranger. Your penalty will be light if you suffer us to arrest you without resort to our swords. But if you should kill one of us you will be imprisoned for life, working in the mason's yards dragging great stones hither and yon with a whip to make you work harder. . . ."

"I will kill all of you if this sword's unsheathed," Elric promised. "Know you that I am Prince Elric of Melniboné and I bear the Black Sword!"

The captain's red face blanched. Then he straightened his shoulders. "Nonetheless I must perform my duty. Men—"

"What is this undignified altercation? Captain, are you aware that you address my friend Prince Elric?"

The captain turned, evidently in relief, to stare at the newcomer who had just ridden up. He was a man of about forty with a square, handsome face, dressed in gilded armor over which was arranged a white cloak. A helm crested with scarlet feathers was on his head. It was the man who had recognized Elric earlier that day. But Elric had never seen him before.

"He cannot pay the Traveler's Tax, my lord," the captain said weakly. "I had no choice but to . . ."

The horseman drew a small purse from his belt and flung it to land at the captain's feet. "There is the tax—and more."

The captain of the Watch bent and picked up the purse. He opened it and peered inside. "Thank you, my lord. Come, men." Hastily he backed away and returned to where he had left his horse. The Watch rode off leaving Elric looking at the man in gilded armor, who smiled at the albino's surprise.

"I thank you, sir," said Elric. "I had no wish to kill them. But . . ."

The knight gestured toward Elric's horse. "Will you mount and ride with me? I would be honored if you would be my guest for this night."

"I am not one who seeks charity, sir."

"I know that, my lord. It is I who seek your aid. I have been searching for you for several months."

"What is the nature of the aid you desire?"

"Perhaps you will allow me to explain that over a meal at the house I have taken in Chalal. It is not too far distant."

Elric liked the look of the man and responded to his courtesy. "Thank you," he said. "I would be grateful." He went to his horse and mounted it. Then they rode off together down the avenue until they came at last to a house with a low wall that was covered in vines of several different hues. They passed through a gate and in the courtyard a groom took their steeds. They entered a door, walked along a short passage and came to a warm, well-lit room where a table had been laid for a meal. Somewhere food was cooking and the smell made Elric realize how little he had eaten recently. At the table one man was already seated. He grinned when he saw Elric and he got up.

"Moonglum!"

"Greetings, Elric. Our host's men sought me out as I haggled with a merchant who seemed unaware of the danger his caravan would face if unprotected by us. I told him where I thought he might find you. I am glad he discovered you so swiftly. I have been waiting to eat for an hour!"

The knight handed his helmet to a servant, and other servants began to divest him of his breastplate and greaves, handing him a loose brocade robe, which he put on.

As they seated themselves he said, "I am Duke Avan Astran of Old Hrolmar in Vilmir."

"I have heard of you, my lord." Elric helped himself to the salad offered him by a servant. Duke Avan Astran was known as a great adventurer whose journeyings across the world had made his city rich. "You are famous for your travels."

52

Duke Avan smiled. "Aye. I have explored most of the world. I have been to your own Melniboné and I have ventured East to Master Moonglum's lands—to Elwher and the Unknown Kingdoms. I have been to Myyrrhn, where the Winged Folk live. I have traveled as far as World's Edge and hope one day to go beyond. But I have never crossed the Boiling Sea and I know only a small stretch of coast along the Western Continent that has no name. You have been there, I believe?"

"I was there once, when the Sea Lords made their fateful massing, but I have not been there since."

"Would you go there?"

"There is nothing to make me wish to do so."

From across the table Elric glanced at Moonglum's face, which had suddenly become alert, almost worried. He looked at Duke Avan's expression and tried to decipher it. He returned his attention to his food.

"You have never explored the interior of the Western Continent?" Duke Avan continued.

"No."

"And yet you know there is some evidence that your own ancestors originally came from that mainland?"

"Evidence? A few legends, that is all."

"One of those legends speaks of a city older than dreaming Imrryr. A city that still exists in the deep jungles of the west."

"You mean R'lin K'ren A'a?" Elric pretended a lack of interest he no longer felt.

"Aye. A strange name. You pronounce it more fluently than could I."

"It means simply 'Where the High Ones Meet' in the ancient speech of Melniboné."

"So I have read."

"And," Elric cut into veal in a rich, sweet sauce, "it does not exist."

"It is marked on a map I have."

53

Deliberately Elric chewed his meat and swallowed it. "The map is doubtless a forgery."

"Perhaps. Do you recall anything else of the legend of R'lin K'ren A'a?"

"There is the story of the Creature Doomed to Live." Elric pushed the food aside and poured wine for himself. "The city is said to have received its name because the Lords of the Higher Worlds once met there to decide the rules of the Cosmic Struggle. They were overheard by the one inhabitant of the city who had not flown when they came. When they discovered him they doomed him to remain alive forever, carrying the frightful knowledge in his head. . . ."

"I have heard that story too. But the one that interests me is that the inhabitants of R'lin K'ren A'a never returned to their city. Instead they struck northwards and crossed the sea. Some reached an island we now call Sorcerer's Isle, while others went further—blown by a great storm—and came at length to a larger island inhabited by dragons whose venom caused all it touched to burn—to Melniboné, in fact."

"And you wish to test the truth of that story. Your interest is that of a scholar?"

Duke Avan laughed. "Partly. But my main interest in R'lin K'ren A'a is more materialistic. For your ancestors left a great treasure behind them when they fled their city. Particularly they abandoned an image of Arioch, the Lord of Chaos—a monstrous image, carved in jade, whose eyes were two huge, identical gems of a kind unknown anywhere else in all the lands of the Earth. Jewels from another plane of existence. Jewels which could reveal all the secrets of the Higher Worlds, of the past and the future, of the myriad planes of the cosmos. . . ."

"All cultures have similar legends. Wishful thinking, Duke Avan, that is all. . . ."

"But the Melnibonéans had a culture unlike any others. The

54

Melnibonéans are not true men, as you well know. Their powers are superior, their knowledge far greater. . . ."

"It was once thus," Elric said. "But that great power and knowledge is not mine. I have only a fragment of it. . . ."

"I did not seek you in Bakshaan and later in Jadmar because I believed you could verify what I have heard. I did not cross the sea to Filkhar, then to Argimiliar and at last to Pikarayd because I thought you would instantly confirm all that I have spoken of—I sought you because I think you the only man who would wish to accompany me on a voyage which would give us the truth or falsehood to these legends once and for all."

Elric tilted his head and drained his winecup.

"Cannot you do that for yourself? Why should you desire my company on the expedition? From what I have heard of you, Duke Avan, you are not one who needs support in his venturings. . . ."

Duke Avan laughed. "I went alone to Elwher when my men deserted me in the Weeping Waste. It is not in my nature to know physical fear. But I have survived my travels this long because I have shown proper foresight and caution before setting off. Now it seems I must face dangers I cannot anticipate—sorcery, perhaps. It struck me, therefore, that I needed an ally who had some experience of fighting sorcery. And since I would have no truck with the ordinary kind of wizard such as Pan Tang spawns, you were my only choice. You are a wanderer, Prince Elric, just as I am. You were a wanderer before Imrryr fell, as well as after. Indeed, if it had not been for your yearning to travel, your cousin would never have usurped the Ruby Throne of Melniboné while you were absent. . . ."

"Enough of that," Elric said bitterly. "Let's talk of this expedition. Where is the map?"

"You will accompany me?"

"Show me the map."

Duke Avan drew a scroll from his pouch. "Here it is."

"Where did you find it?"

"On Melniboné."

"You have been there recently?" Elric felt anger rise in him.

Duke Avan raised a hand. "Many have come and gone amongst the ruins of Imrryr since she fell, my lord. Most sought treasure. I sought, in that particular case, knowledge. I found a casket which had been sealed, it seemed, for an eternity. Within that casket was this map." He spread out the scroll on the table. Elric recognized the style and the script—the old High Speech of Melniboné. It was a map of part of the Western Continent—more than he had ever seen on any other map. It showed a great river winding into the interior for a hundred miles or more. The river appeared to flow through a jungle and then divide into two rivers which later rejoined. The island of land thus formed had a black circle marked on it. Against this circle, in the involved writing of ancient Melniboné, was the name R'lin K'ren A'a. Elric inspected the scroll carefully. It did not seem to be a forgery.

"Is this all you found?" he asked.

"The scroll was sealed and this was imbedded in the seal," Duke Avan said, handing something to Elric.

Elric held the object in his palm. It was a tiny ruby of a red so deep as to seem black at first, but when he turned it into the light he saw an image at the center of the ruby and he recognized that image. He frowned, then he said, "I will agree to your proposal, Duke Avan. Will you let me keep this?"

"Do you know what it is?"

"No. But I should like to find out. There is a memory somewhere in my mind. . . ."

"Very well, take it. I will keep the map."

"When did you have it in mind to set off?"

"We'll ride to the coast tomorrow. My ship awaits us. From there we sail round the southern coast to the Boiling Sea."

"There are few who have returned from that ocean," Elric murmured sardonically. He glanced across the table and saw that Moonglum was imploring with his eyes for Elric not to have any part of

56

Duke Avan's scheme. Elric smiled at his friend. "The adventure is to my taste."

Miserably Moonglum shrugged.

2

THE COAST OF Lormyr disappeared in warm mist and the Vilmirian schooner dipped its graceful prow toward the west and the Boiling Sea.

Only once before had Elric ventured into this sea and then he had flown high above it on a bird of gold and silver and brass, seeking the bleak island on which stood the magical palace of Ashanaloon—Myshella's palace. Standing in the poop Elric stared ahead into the writhing mist and tried not to think of Myshella and the dreams and emotions she had awakened within him. He wiped sweat from his face and turned to see Moonglum's worried countenance.

"You still keep patience with me, Master Moonglum. Your warnings are always well founded and yet I never heed them. I wonder why that is."

Moonglum raised his gloomy eyes to regard the taut sails of the schooner. "Because you desire danger as other men desire love-making or drinking—for in danger you find forgetfulness."

"Do I? Few of the dangers we have faced together have helped me forget. Rather they have strengthened my memories, improved the quality of my sorrow. . . ." Elric drew a deep, melancholy breath. "I go where the danger is because I think that an answer might lie there—some reason for all this tragedy and paradox. Yet I know I shall never find it."

57

"Yet that is why you sail to R'lin K'ren A'a, is it not? You hope that your remote ancestors had the answer you want."

"R'lin K'ren A'a is a myth. Even should the map prove genuine, what shall we find but a few ruins? Imrryr stood for ten thousand years and she was built at least two centuries after my people settled on Melniboné. Time will have taken R'lin K'ren A'a away."

"And the Jade Man?"

"If the statue ever existed it could have been looted at any time in the past hundred centuries."

"And the Creature Doomed to Live?"

"A myth."

"But you hope that it is all as Duke Avan says. . . ."

"No, Moonglum—I *fear* that it is all as he says."

The wind blew whimsically and the schooner's passage was slow as the heat grew greater. The crew sweated and murmured fearfully and upon each face was a stricken look. Only Duke Avan seemed to retain his confidence. He called to his men to take heart, that they should all be rich soon, and he gave orders for the oars to be unshipped. The men stripped down to man them, revealing skins as red as those of a cooked lobster. Duke Avan made a joke of that. The Vilmirians did not laugh.

Around the ship the sea bubbled and roared, and they navigated by their crude instruments alone, for the steam obscured everything. Once a green thing erupted from the sea and glared at them before disappearing.

They ate and slept little and Elric rarely left the poop. Moonglum bore the heat silently and Duke Avan went about the ship encouraging his men, seemingly oblivious of the discomfort.

"After all," he pointed out to Moonglum, "we are only crossing the outer reaches of the sea. Think what it must be like at the middle."

"I would rather not. I fear I'll be boiled to death before another day has passed."

"Nonsense, friend Moonglum, the steam is good for you. There is nothing healthier!" Duke Avan stretched, seemingly with pleasure. "It cleans all the poisons from the system."

Moonglum offered him a withering look, and Avan grinned. "Be of better cheer, Master Moonglum. According to my charts—such as they are—a couple of days will see us nearing the coasts of the Western Continent."

"The thought fails to raise my spirits very greatly," Moonglum said, and went to find his cabin.

But shortly thereafter the sea grew slowly less frenetic and the steam began to disperse and the heat became more tolerable, until at last they emerged into a calm ocean beneath a blue sky in which hung the golden sun. The spirits of the crew rose and they buried the three men who had succumbed on a little yellow island, where they found fruit and a spring of fresh water. While they lay at anchor off the island Duke Avan called Elric to his cabin and showed him the ancient map.

"See! This island is marked there. The map's scale seems reasonably accurate. Another three days and we shall be at the mouth of the river."

Elric nodded. "But it would be wise to rest here for a while until our strength is fully restored and the morale of the crew is higher. There are reasons, after all, why men have avoided the jungles of the west over the centuries."

"Certainly there are savages there—some say they are not even human—but I'm confident we can deal with those dangers. I have much experience of strange territories, Prince Elric."

"But you said yourself you feared other dangers."

"True. Very well, we'll do as you suggest."

On the fourth day a strong wind began to blow from the east and they raised anchor. The schooner leapt over the waves under only half her canvas and the crew saw this as a good omen.

"They are mindless fools," Moonglum said as they stood clinging to the rigging in the prow. "The time will come when they will wish they were suffering the cleaner hardships of the Boiling Sea. This journey, Elric, will benefit none of us, even if the riches of R'lin K'ren A'a are still there."

But Elric did not answer. He was lost in strange thoughts, unusual thoughts for him, for he was remembering his childhood, his mother and his father. They had been the last true rulers of the Bright Empire—proud, insouciant, cruel. They had expected him—perhaps because of his strange albinism—to restore the glories of Melniboné. Instead he had destroyed what had been left of that glory. They, like himself, had had no real place in this new age of the Young Kingdoms, but they had refused to acknowledge it. This journey to the Western Continent, to the land of his ancestors, had a peculiar attraction for him. Here no new nations had emerged. The Continent had, as far as he knew, remained the same since R'lin K'ren A'a had been abandoned. The jungles would be the jungles his folk had known, the land would be the land that had given birth to his peculiar race, molded the character of its people with their somber pleasures, their melancholy arts and their dark delights. Had his ancestors felt this agony of knowledge, this impotence in the face of the understanding that existence had no point, no purpose, no hope? Was this why they had built their civilization in that particular pattern, why they had disdained the more placid, spiritual values of mankind's philosophers? He knew that many of the intellectuals of the Young Kingdoms pitied the powerful folk of Melniboné as mad. But if they had been mad and if they had imposed a madness upon the world that had lasted a hundred centuries, what had made them so? Perhaps the secret did lie in R'lin K'ren A'a—not in any tangible form, but in the ambience created by the dark jungles and the deep, old rivers. Perhaps here, at last, he would be able to feel at one with himself.

He ran his fingers through his milk-white hair and there was a kind of innocent anguish in his crimson eyes. He was the last of his kind and yet he was unlike his kind. Moonglum had been wrong. Elric knew that everything that existed had its opposite. In danger he might find peace. And yet, of course, in peace there was danger. Being an imperfect creature in an imperfect world he would always know paradox. And that was why in paradox there was always a kind of truth. That was why philosophers and soothsayers flourished. In a perfect world there would be no place for them. In an imperfect world the mysteries were always without solution, and that was why there was always a great choice of solutions.

It was on the morning of the third day that the coast was sighted, and the schooner steered her way through the sandbanks of the great delta and anchored, at last, at the mouth of the dark and nameless river.

3

EVENING CAME AND the sun began to set over the black outlines of the massive trees. A rich, ancient smell came from the jungle, and through the twilight echoed the cries of strange birds and beasts. Elric was impatient to begin the quest up the river. Sleep—never welcome—was now impossible to achieve. He stood unmoving on the deck, his eyes hardly blinking, his brain barely active, as if expecting something to happen to him. The rays of the sun stained his face and threw black shadows over the deck, and then it was dark and still under the moon and the stars. He wanted the jungle to absorb him. He wanted to be one with the trees and the shrubs and the creeping beasts. He wanted thought to disappear. He drew the heavily scented air into his lungs as if that alone would make him become what at that moment he desired to be. The drone of insects became a murmuring voice that called him into the heart of the old, old forest. And yet he could not move—could not answer. And at length Moonglum came up on deck and touched his shoulder and said something, and passively he went below to his bunk and wrapped himself in his cloak and lay there, still listening to the voice of the jungle.

Even Duke Avan seemed in a more introspective mood than usual when they upped anchor the next morning and began to row against the sluggish current. There were few gaps in the foliage above their heads and they had the impression that they were entering a huge, gloomy tunnel, leaving the sunlight behind with the sea. Bright plants twined among the vines that hung from the leafy canopy and caught in the ship's masts as they moved. Ratlike animals with long arms swung through the branches and peered at them with bright, knowing eyes. The river turned and the sea was no longer in sight. Shafts of sunlight filtered down to the deck and the light had a greenish tinge to it. Elric became more alert than he had ever been since he agreed to accompany Duke Avan. He took a keen interest in every detail of the jungle and of the black river, over which moved swarms of insects like agitated clouds of mist and in which blossoms drifted like drops of blood in ink. Everywhere were rustlings, sudden squawks, barks and wet noises made by fish or river animals as they hunted the prey disturbed by the ship's oars, which cut into the great clumps of weed and sent the things that hid there scurrying. The others began to complain of insect bites, but Elric was not troubled by them, perhaps because no insect could desire his deficient blood.

Duke Avan passed him on the deck. The Vilmirian slapped at his forehead. "You seem more cheerful, Prince Elric."

Elric smiled absently. "Perhaps I am."

"I must admit I personally find all this a bit oppressive. I'll be glad when we reach the city."

"You are still convinced you'll find it?"

"I'll be convinced otherwise when I've explored every inch of the island we're bound for."

So absorbed had he become in the atmosphere of the jungle that Elric was hardly aware of the ship or his companions. The ship beat very slowly up the river, moving at little more than walking speed.

A few days passed but Elric scarcely noticed, for the jungle did not change—and then the river widened and the canopy parted and the wide, hot sky was suddenly full of huge birds crowding upward as the ship disturbed them. All but Elric were pleased to be under the open sky again, and spirits rose. Elric went below.

The attack on the ship came some days later. There was a whistling noise and a scream, and a sailor writhed and fell over clutching at a gray, thin semicircle of something which had buried itself in his stomach. An upper yard came crashing to the deck, bringing sail and rigging with it. A headless body took four paces toward the poop deck before collapsing, the blood pumping from the obscene hole that was its neck. And everywhere was the thin whistling noise. Elric heard the sounds from below and came up instantly, buckling on his sword. The first face he saw was Moonglum's. The red-haired man looked terrified and was crouching against a rail on the starboard side. Elric had the impression of gray blurs whistling past, slashing into flesh and rigging, wood and canvas. Some fell to the deck and he saw that they were thin discs of crystalline rock, about a foot in diameter. They were being hurled from both banks of the river and there was no protection against them.

He tried to see who was throwing the discs and glimpsed something moving in the trees along the right bank. Then the discs ceased suddenly, and there was a pause before some of the sailors dashed across the deck to seek better cover. Duke Avan suddenly appeared in the stern. He had unsheathed his sword.

"Get below. Get your bucklers and any armor you can find. Bring bows. Arm yourselves, men, or you're finished."

And as he spoke their attackers broke from the trees and began to wade into the water. No more discs came, and it seemed likely they had exhausted their supply.

"By Chardros!" Avan gasped. "Are these real creatures or some sorcerer's conjurings?"

The things were essentially reptilian but with feathery crests and neck wattles, though their faces were almost human. Their forelegs were like the arms and hands of men, but their hindlegs were incredibly long and storklike. Balanced on these legs, their bodies towered over the water. They carried great clubs in which slits had been cut, and doubtless these were what they used to hurl the crystalline discs. Staring at their faces, Elric was horrified. In some subtle way they reminded him of the characteristic faces of his own folk—the folk of Melniboné. Were these creatures his cousins? Or were they a species from which his people had evolved? He stopped asking the questions as an intense hatred for the creatures filled him. They were obscene: sight of them brought bile into his throat. Without thinking he drew Stormbringer from its sheath.

The Black Sword began to howl and the familiar black radiance spilled from it. The runes carved into its blade pulsed a vivid scarlet, which turned slowly to a deep purple and then to black once more.

The creatures were wading through the water on their stiltlike legs and they paused when they saw the sword, glancing at one another. And they were not the only ones unnerved by the sight, for Duke Avan and his men paled too.

"Gods!" Avan yelled. "I know not which I prefer the look of—those who attack us or that which defends us!"

"Stay well away from that sword," Moonglum warned. "It has the habit of killing those its master likes best."

And now the reptilian savages were upon them, clutching at the ship's rails as the armed sailors rushed back on deck to meet the attack.

Clubs came at Elric from all sides, but Stormbringer shrieked

64

and parried each blow. He held the sword in both hands, whirling it this way and that, ploughing great gashes in the scaly bodies.

The creatures hissed and opened red mouths in agony and rage while their thick, black blood sank into the waters of the river. Although from the legs upward they were only slightly larger than a tall, well-built man, they had more vitality than any human, and the deepest cuts hardly seemed to affect them, even when administered by Stormbringer. Elric was astonished at this resistance to the sword's power. Often a nick was enough for the sword to draw a man's soul from him. These things seemed immune. Perhaps they had no souls. . . .

He fought on, his hatred giving him strength.

But elsewhere on the ship the sailors were being routed. Rails were torn off and the great clubs crushed planks and brought down more rigging. The savages were intent on destroying the ship as well as the crew. And there was little doubt, now, that they would not be successful.

Avan shouted to Elric. "By the names of all the Gods, Prince Elric, can you not summon some further sorcery? We are doomed else!"

Elric knew Avan spoke truth. All around him the ship was being gradually pulled apart by the hissing reptilian creatures. Most of them had sustained horrible wounds from the defenders, but only one or two had collapsed. Elric began to suspect that they did, in fact, fight supernatural enemies.

He backed away and sought shelter beneath a half-crushed doorway as he tried to concentrate on a method of calling upon supernatural aid.

He was panting with exhaustion and clung to a beam as the ship rocked back and forth in the water. He fought to clear his head.

And then the incantation came to him. He was not sure if it was appropriate, but it was the only one he could recall. His ancestors had made pacts, thousands of years before, with all the elementals who controlled the animal world. In the past he had summoned help from various of these spirits, but never from the one he now sought to call. From his mouth began to issue the ancient, beautiful and convoluted words of Melniboné's High Speech.

"King With Wings! Lord of all that work and are not seen, upon whose labors all else depends! Nnuuurrrr'c'c of the Insect Folk, I summon thee!"

Save for the motion of the ship, Elric ceased to be aware of all else happening around him. The sounds of the fight dimmed and were heard no more as he sent his voice out beyond his plane of the Earth into another—the plane dominated by King Nnuuurrrr'c'c of the Insects, paramount lord of his people.

In his ears now Elric heard a buzzing, and gradually the buzzing formed itself in words.

"Who art thou, mortal? What right hast thee to summon me?"

"I am Elric, last ruler of Melniboné. My ancestors aided thee, Nnuuurrrr'c'c."

"Aye—but long ago."

"And it is long ago that they last called on thee for thine aid!"

"True. What aid dost thou now require, Elric of Melniboné?"

"Look upon my plane. Thou wilt see that I am in danger. Canst thou abolish this danger, friend of the Insects?"

Now a filmy shape formed and could be seen as if through several layers of cloudy silk. Elric tried to keep his eyes upon it, but it kept leaving his field of vision and then returning for a few moments. He knew that he looked into another plane of the Earth.

"Canst thou help me, Nnuuurrrr'c'c?"

"Hast thou no patron of thine own species? Some Lord of Chaos who can aid thee?"

"My patron is Arioch and he is a temperamental demon at best. These days he aids me little."

"Then I must send thee allies, mortal. But call upon me no more when this is done."

"I shall not summon thee again, Nnuuurrrr'c'c."

The layers of film disappeared and with them the shape.

The noise of the battle crashed once again on Elric's conscious-

66

ness, and he heard with sharper clarity than before the screams of the sailors and the hissing of the reptilian savages. And when he looked out from his shelter he saw that at least half the crew was dead.

As he came on deck Moonglum rushed up. "I thought you slain, Elric! What became of you?" He was plainly relieved to see his friend still lived.

"I sought aid from another plane—but it does not seem to have materialized."

"I'm thinking we're doomed and had best try to swim downstream and seek a hiding place in the jungle," Moonglum said.

"What of Duke Avan? Is he dead?"

"He lives. But those creatures are all but impervious to our weapons. This ship will sink ere long." Moonglum lurched as the deck tilted and he reached out to grab a trailing rope, letting his long sword dangle by its wrist-thong. "They are not attacking the stern at present. We can slip into the water there. . . ."

"I made a bargain with Duke Avan," Elric reminded the Eastlander. "I cannot desert him."

"Then we'll all perish!"

"What's that?" Elric bent his head, listening intently.

"I hear nothing."

It was a whine which deepened in tone until it became a drone. Now Moonglum heard it also and looked about him, seeking the source of the sound. And suddenly he gasped, pointing upward. "Is that the aid you sought?"

There was a vast cloud of them, black against the blue of the sky. Every so often the sun would flash off a color—a rich blue, green or red. They came spiraling down toward the ship, and now both sides fell silent, staring skyward.

The flying things were like huge dragonflies and the brightness and richness of their coloring was breathtaking. It was their wings that made the droning sound, which now began to increase in loudness and heighten in pitch as the huge insects sped nearer.

Realizing that they were the object of the attack, the reptile men stumbled backward on their long legs, trying to reach the shore before the gigantic insects were upon them.

But it was too late for flight.

The dragonflies settled on the savages until nothing could be seen of their bodies. The hissing increased and sounded almost pitiful as the insects bore their victims down to the surface and then inflicted on them whatever terrible death it was. Perhaps they stung with their tails—it was not possible for the watchers to see.

Sometimes a storklike leg would emerge from the water and thrash in the air for a moment. But soon, just as the reptiles were covered by the insect bodies, so were their cries drowned by the strange and blood-chilling humming that arose on all sides.

A sweating Duke Avan, sword still in hand, ran up the deck. "Is this your doing, Prince Elric?"

Elric looked on with satisfaction, but the others were plainly disgusted. "It was," he said.

"Then I thank you for your aid. This ship is holed in a dozen places and is letting in water at a terrible rate. It's a wonder we have not yet sunk. I've given orders to begin rowing and I hope we make it to the island in time." He pointed upstream. "There, you can just see it."

"What if there are more of those savages there?" Moonglum asked.

Avan smiled grimly, indicating the farther shore. "Look." On their peculiar legs a dozen or more of the reptiles were fleeing into the jungle, having witnessed the fate of their comrades. "They'll be reluctant to attack us again, I think."

Now the huge dragonflies were rising into the air again, and Avan turned away as he glimpsed what they had left behind. "By the Gods, you work fierce sorcery, Prince Elric! Ugh!"

Elric smiled and shrugged. "It is effective, Duke Avan." He sheathed his runesword. It seemed reluctant to enter the scabbard and it moaned as if in resentment.

Moonglum glanced at it. "That blade will want to feast soon, Elric, whether you desire it or not."

"Doubtless it will find something to feed on in the forest," said the albino. He stepped over a piece of broken mast and went below.

Moonglum looked at the new scum on the surface of the water and he shuddered.

4

THE WRECKED SCHOONER was almost awash when the crew clambered overboard with lines and began the task of dragging it up the mud that formed the banks of the island. Before them was a wall of foliage that seemed impenetrable. Moonglum followed Elric, lowering himself into the shallows. They began to wade ashore.

As they left the water and set foot on the hard, baked earth, Moonglum stared at the forest. No wind moved the branches and a peculiar silence had descended. No birds called from the trees, no insects buzzed, there were none of the barks and cries of animals they had heard on their journey up-river.

"Those supernatural friends of yours seem to have frightened more than the savages away," Moonglum murmured. "This place seems lifeless."

Elric nodded. "It is strange."

Duke Avan joined them. He had discarded his finery—ruined in the fight, anyway—and now wore a padded leather jerkin and doe-skin breeks. His sword was at his side. "We'll have to leave most of our men behind with the ship," he said regretfully. "They'll make what repairs they can while we press on to find R'lin K'ren A'a." He drew his light cloak about him. "Is it my imagination, or is there an odd atmosphere?"

"We have already remarked on it," Moonglum said. "All life seems to have fled the island."

Duke Avan grinned. "If all we face is as timid, we have nothing further to fear. I must admit, Prince Elric, that if I had wished you harm and then seen you conjure those monsters from thin air, I'd think twice about getting too close to you! Thank you, by the way, for what you did. We should have perished by now if it had not been for you."

"It was for my aid that you asked me to accompany you," Elric said wearily. "Let's eat and rest and then continue with our expedition."

A shadow passed over Duke Avan's face then. Something in Elric's manner had disturbed him.

Entering the jungle was no easy matter. Armed with axes, the six members of the crew (all that could be spared) began to hack at the undergrowth. And still the unnatural silence prevailed. . . .

By nightfall they were less than half a mile into the forest and completely exhausted. The forest was so thick that there was barely room to pitch their tent. The only light in the camp came from the small, sputtering fire outside the tent. The crewmen slept where they could in the open.

Elric could not sleep; but now it was not the jungle which kept him awake. He was puzzled by the silence, for he was sure that it was not their presence which had driven all life away. There was not a single small rodent, bird or insect anywhere to be seen. There were no traces of animal life. The island had been deserted of all but vegetation for a long while—perhaps for centuries or tens of centuries. He remembered another part of the old legend of R'lin K'ren A'a. It had been said that when the Gods came to meet there, not only the citizens fled, but also all the wildlife. Nothing had dared see the High Lords or listen to their conversation. Elric shivered, turning his white head this way and that on the rolled cloak that supported it, his crimson eyes tortured. If there were dangers on this island, they would be subtler dangers than those they had faced on the river.

The noise of their passage through the forest was the only sound to be heard on the island as they forced their way on the next morning.

With lodestone in one hand and map in the other, Duke Avan Astran sought to guide them, directing his men where to cut their path. But the going became even slower, and it was obvious that no creatures had come this way for many ages.

By the fourth day they had reached a natural clearing of flat volcanic rock and found a spring there. Gratefully they made camp. Elric began to wash his face in the cool water when he heard a yell behind him. He sprang up. One of the crewmen was reaching for an arrow and fitting it to his bow.

"What is it?" Duke Avan called.

"I saw something, my lord!"

"Nonsense, there are no—"

"Look!" The man drew back the string and let fly into the upper terraces of the forest. Something did seem to stir then, and Elric thought he saw a flash of gray among the trees.

"Did you see what kind of creature it was?" Moonglum asked the man.

"No, master. I feared at first it was those reptiles again."

"They're too frightened to follow us onto this island," Duke Avan reassured him.

"I hope you're right," Moonglum said nervously.

"Then what could it have been?" Elric wondered.

"I—I thought it was a man, master," the crewman stuttered.

Elric stared thoughtfully into the trees. "A man?"

Moonglum knew his friend well. "You were hoping for this, Elric?"

"I am not sure. . . ."

Duke Avan shrugged. "More likely the shadow of a cloud passing over the trees. According to my calculations we should have reached the city by now."

"You think, after all, that it does not exist?" Elric said.

"I am beginning not to care, Prince Elric." The duke leaned against the bole of a huge tree, brushing aside a vine which touched his face. "Still there's nought else to do. The ship won't be ready to sail yet." He looked up into the branches. "I did not think I should miss those damned insects that plagued us on our way here. . . ."

The crewman who had shot the arrow suddenly shouted again. "There! I saw him! It is a man!"

While the others stared but failed to discern anything, Duke Avan continued to lean against the tree. "You saw nothing. There is nothing here to see."

Elric turned toward him. "Give me the map and the lodestone, Duke Avan. I have a feeling I can find the way."

The Vilmirian shrugged, an expression of doubt on his square, handsome face. He handed the things over to Elric.

They rested the night and in the morning they continued, with Elric leading the way.

And at noon they broke out of the forest and saw the ruins of R'lin K'ren A'a.

5

NOTHING GREW AMONG the ruins of the city. The streets were broken and the walls of the houses had fallen, but there were no weeds flowering in the cracks and it seemed that the city had but recently been brought down by an earthquake. Only one thing still stood intact, towering over the ruins. It was a gigantic statue of white, gray and green jade—the statue of a naked youth with a face of almost feminine beauty that turned sightless eyes toward the north.

"The eyes!" Duke Avan Astran said. "They're gone!"

The others said nothing as they stared at the statue and the ruins surrounding it. The area was relatively small and the buildings had had little decoration. The inhabitants seemed to have been a simple, well-to-do folk—totally unlike the Melnibonéans of the Bright Empire. Elric could not believe that the people of R'lin K'ren A'a had been his ancestors. They had been too sane.

"The statue's already been looted," Duke Avan continued. "Our damned journey's been in vain!"

Elric laughed. "Did you really think you would be able to prise the Jade Man's eyes from their sockets, my lord?"

The statue was as tall as any tower of the Dreaming City and the head alone must have been the size of a reasonably large building. Duke Avan pursed his lips and refused to listen to Elric's mocking voice. "We may yet find the journey worth our while," he said. "There were other treasures in R'lin K'ren A'a. Come. . . ."

He led the way into the city.

Very few of the buildings were even partially standing but they were nonetheless fascinating, if only for the peculiar nature of their building materials, which were of a kind the travelers had never seen before.

The colors were many but faded by time—soft reds and yellows and blues—and they flowed together to make almost infinite combinations.

Elric reached out to touch one wall and was surprised at the cool feel of the smooth material. It was neither stone nor wood nor metal. Perhaps it had been brought here from another plane?

He tried to visualize the city as it had been before it was deserted. The streets had been wide, there had been no surrounding wall, the houses had been low and built around large courtyards. If this was, indeed, the original home of his people, what had happened to change them from the peaceful citizens of R'lin K'ren A'a to the insane builders of Imrryr's bizarre and dreaming towers? Elric had thought he might find a solution to a mystery here, but instead he had found another mystery. It was his fate, he thought, shrugging to himself.

And then the first crystal disc hummed past his head and smashed against a collapsing wall.

The next disc split the skull of a crewman, and a third nicked Moonglum's ear before they had thrown themselves flat amongst the rubble.

"They're vengeful, those creatures," Avan said with a hard smile. "They'll risk much to pay us back for their comrades' deaths!"

Terror was on the face of each surviving crewman, and fear had begun to creep into Avan's eyes.

More discs clattered nearby, but it was plain that the party was temporarily out of sight of the reptiles. Moonglum coughed as white dust rose from the rubble and caught in his throat.

"You'd best summon those monstrous friends of yours again, Elric."

Elric shook his head. "I cannot. My ally said he would not serve me a second time." He looked to his left where the four walls of a small house still stood. There seemed to be no door, only a window.

"Then call Arioch," Moonglum said urgently. "Anything."

"Arioch? I am not sure . . ."

Then Elric rolled over and sprang for the shelter, flinging himself through the window to land on a pile of masonry, which grazed his hands and knees.

He staggered upright. In the distance he could see the huge, blind statue of the god dominating the city. This was said to be an image of Arioch—though it resembled no image of Arioch Elric had ever seen manifested. Did that image protect R'lin K'ren A'a—or did it threaten it? Someone screamed. He glanced through the opening and saw that a disc had landed and chopped through a man's forearm.

He drew Stormbringer and raised it, facing the jade statue.

74

"Arioch!" he cried. "Arioch—aid me!"

Black light burst from the blade and it began to sing, as if joining in Elric's incantation.

"Arioch!"

Would the demon come? Of late the patron of the Kings of Melniboné had refused to materialize, claiming that more urgent business called him—business concerning the eternal struggle between Law and Chaos.

"Arioch!"

Sword and man were now wreathed in a palpitating black mist and Elric's white face was flung back, seeming to writhe as the mist writhed.

"Arioch! I beg thee to aid me! It is Elric who calls thee!"

And then a voice reached his ears. It was a soft, purring, reasonable voice. It was a tender voice.

"Elric, I am fondest of thee. I love thee more than any other mortal—but aid thee I cannot—not yet."

Elric cried desperately: "Then we are doomed to perish here!"

"Thou canst escape this danger. Flee alone into the forest. Leave the others while thou hast time. Thou hast a destiny to fulfill elsewhere and elsewhen. . . ."

"I will not desert them."

"Thou art foolish, sweet Elric."

"Arioch—since Melniboné's founding thou hast aided her kings. Aid her last king this day!"

"I cannot dissipate my energies. A great struggle looms. And it would cost me much to return to R'lin K'ren A'a. Flee now. Thou shalt be saved. Only the others will die."

And then the Duke of Hell had gone. Elric sensed the passing of his presence. He frowned, fingering his belt-pouch, trying to recall something he had once heard. Slowly he resheathed the reluctant sword. Then there was a thump and Moonglum stood panting before him.

"Well, is aid on the way?"

"I fear not." Elric shook his head in despair. "Once again Arioch refuses me. Once again he speaks of a greater destiny—a need to conserve his strength."

"Your ancestors could have picked a more tractable demon as their patron. Our reptilian friends are closing in. Look . . ." Moonglum pointed to the outskirts of the city. A band of about a dozen stilt-legged creatures were advancing, their huge clubs at the ready.

There was a scuffling noise from the rubble on the other side of the wall and Avan appeared, leading his men through the opening. He was cursing.

"No extra aid is coming, I fear," Elric told him.

The Vilmirian smiled grimly. "Then the monsters out there knew more than did we!"

"It seems so."

"We'll have to try to hide from them," Moonglum said without much conviction. "We'd not survive a fight."

The little party left the ruined house and began to inch its way through what cover it could find, moving gradually nearer to the center of the city and the statue of the Jade Man.

A sharp hiss from behind them told them that the reptile warriors had sighted them again, and another Vilmirian fell with a crystal disc protruding from his back. They broke into a panicky run.

Ahead now was a red building of several stories which still had its roof.

"In there!" Duke Avan shouted.

With some relief they dashed unhesitatingly up worn steps and through a series of dusty passages until they paused to catch their breath in a great, gloomy hall.

The hall was completely empty and a little light filtered through cracks in the wall.

"This place has lasted better than the others," Duke Avan said. "I wonder what its function was. A fortress, perhaps."

"They seem not to have been a warlike race," Moonglum pointed out. "I suspect the building had some other function."

The three surviving crewmen were looking fearfully about them. They looked as if they would have preferred to face the reptile warriors outside.

Elric began to cross the floor and then paused as he saw something painted on the far wall.

Moonglum saw it too. "What's that, friend Elric?"

Elric recognized the symbols as the written High Speech of old Melniboné, but it was subtly different and it took him a short time to decipher its meaning.

"Know you what it says, Elric?" Duke Avan murmured, joining them.

"Aye—but it's cryptic enough. It says: 'If thou hast come to slay me, then thou art welcome. If thou hast come without the means to awaken the Jade Man, then begone."

"Is it addressed to us, I wonder," Avan mused, "or has it been there for a long while?"

Elric shrugged. "It could have been inscribed at any time during the past ten thousand years. . . ."

Moonglum walked up to the wall and reached out to touch it. "I would say it was fairly recent," he said. "The paint is still wet."

Elric frowned. "Then there are inhabitants here still. Why do they not reveal themselves?"

"Could those reptiles out there be the denizens of R'lin K'ren A'a?" Avan said. "There is nothing in the legends which says they were humans who fled this place. . . ."

Elric's face clouded and he was about to make an angry reply when Moonglum interrupted.

"Perhaps there is just one inhabitant. Is that what you are thinking, Elric. The Creature Doomed to Live? Those sentiments could be his. . . ."

Elric put his hands to his face and made no answer.

"Come," Avan said. "We've no time to debate on legends." He

strode across the floor and entered another doorway, beginning to descend steps. As he reached the bottom they heard him gasp.

The others joined him and saw that he stood on the threshold of another hall. But this one was ankle deep in fragments of stuff that had been thin leaves of a metallic material with the flexibility of parchment. Around the walls were thousands of small holes, rank upon rank, each with a character painted over it.

"What is it?" Moonglum asked.

Elric stooped and picked up one of the fragments. This had half a Melnibonéan character engraved on it. There had even been an attempt to obliterate this.

"It was a library," he said softly. "The library of my ancestors. Someone has tried to destroy it. These scrolls must have been virtually indestructible, yet a great deal of effort has gone into making them indecipherable." He kicked at the fragments. "Plainly our friend—or friends—is a consistent hater of learning."

"Plainly," Avan said bitterly. "Oh, the *value* of those scrolls to the scholar! All destroyed!"

Elric shrugged. "To Limbo with the scholar—their value to me was quite considerable!"

Moonglum put a hand on his friend's arm, but Elric shrugged it off. "I had hoped . . ."

Moonglum cocked his head. "Those reptiles have followed us into the building, by the sound of it."

They heard the distant sound of strange footsteps in the passages behind them.

The little band moved as silently as it could through the ruined scrolls and crossed the hall until it entered another corridor, which led sharply upward.

Then, suddenly, daylight was visible.

Elric peered ahead. "The corridor has collapsed ahead of us and is blocked, by the look of it. The roof has caved in and we may be able to escape through the hole."

They clambered upward over the fallen stones, glancing warily behind them for signs of their pursuers.

At last they emerged in the central square of the city. On the far sides of this square were placed the feet of the great statue, which now towered high above their heads.

Directly before them were two peculiar constructions which, unlike the rest of the buildings, were completely whole. They were domed and faceted and were made of some glass-like substance which diffracted the rays of the sun.

From below they heard the reptile men advancing down the corridor.

"We'll seek shelter in the nearest of those domes," Elric said. He broke into a trot, leading the way.

The others followed him through the irregularly shaped opening at the base of the dome.

Once inside, however, they hesitated, shielding their eyes and blinking heavily as they tried to discern their way.

"It's like a maze of mirrors!" Moonglum gasped. "By the Gods, I've never seen a better. Was that its function, I wonder."

Corridors seemed to go off in all directions—yet they might be nothing more than reflections of the passage they were in. Cautiously Elric began to continue farther into the maze, the five others following him.

"This smells of sorcery to me," Moonglum muttered as they advanced. "Have we been forced into a trap, I wonder?"

Elric drew his sword. It murmured softly—almost querulously.

Everything shifted suddenly and the shapes of his companions grew dim.

"Moonglum! Duke Avan!"

He heard voices murmuring, but they were not the voices of his friends.

"Moonglum!"

But then the little man faded away altogether and Elric was alone.

HE TURNED AND a wall of red brilliance struck his eyes and blinded him.

He called out and his voice was turned into a dismal wail which mocked him.

He tried to move but he could not tell whether he remained in the same spot or walked a dozen miles.

Now there was someone standing a few yards away, seemingly obscured by a screen of multicolored transparent gems. He stepped forward and made to dash away the screen, but it vanished and he stopped suddenly.

He looked on a face of infinite sorrow.

And the face was his own face, save that the man's coloring was normal and his hair was black.

"What are you?" Elric said thickly.

"I have had many names. One is Erekosë. I have been many men. Perhaps I am all men."

"But you are like me!"

"I am you."

"No!"

The phantom's eyes held tears as it stared in pity at Elric.

"Do not weep for me!" Elric roared. "I need no sympathy from you!"

"Perhaps I weep for myself, for I know our fate."

"And what is that?"

"You would not understand."

"Tell me."

"Ask your gods."

Elric raised his sword. Fiercely he said, "No—I'll have my answer from you!"

And the phantom faded away.

Elric shivered. Now the corridor was populated by a thousand such phantoms. Each murmured a different name. Each wore different clothes. But each had his face, if not his coloring.

"Begone!" he screamed. "Oh Gods, what is this place?"

And at his command they disappeared.

"Elric?"

The albino whirled, sword ready. But it was Duke Avan Astran of Old Hrolmar. He touched his own face with trembling fingers but said levelly: "I must tell you that I believe I am losing my sanity, Prince Elric. . . ."

"What have you seen?"

"Many things. I cannot describe them."

"Where are Moonglum and the others?"

"Doubtless each went his separate way, as we did."

Elric raised Stormbringer and brought the blade crashing against a crystal wall. The Black Sword moaned but the wall merely changed its position.

But through a gap now Elric saw ordinary daylight. "Come, Duke Avan—here is escape!"

Avan, dazed, followed him, and they stepped out of the crystal and found themselves in the central square of R'lin K'ren A'a.

But there were noises. Carts and chariots moved about the square. Stalls were erected on one side. People moved peacefully about. And the Jade Man did not dominate the sky above the city. Here there was no Jade Man at all.

Elric looked at the faces. They were the eldritch features of the folk of Melniboné. Yet these had a different cast to them which he could not at first define. Then he recognized what they had. It was tranquillity. He reached out his hand to touch one of the people.

"Tell me, friend, what year . . . ?"

But the man did not hear him. He walked by.

Elric tried to stop several of the passers-by, but not one could see or hear him.

"How did they lose this peace?" Duke Avan asked wonderingly. "How did they become like you, Prince Elric?"

Elric almost snarled as he turned sharply to face the Vilmirian. "Be silent!"

Duke Avan shrugged. "Perhaps this is merely an illusion."

"Perhaps," Elric said sadly, "but I am sure this is how they lived —until the coming of the High Ones."

"You blame the gods, then?"

"I blame the knowledge that the gods brought."

Duke Avan nodded gravely. "I understand."

He turned back toward the great crystal and then stood listening. "Do you hear that voice, Prince Elric? What is it saying?"

Elric heard the voice. It seemed to be coming from the crystal. It was speaking the old tongue of Melniboné, but with a strange accent. "This way," it said. "This way."

Elric paused. "I have no liking to return there."

Avan said, "What choice have we?"

They stepped together through the entrance.

Again they were in the maze that could be one corridor or many, and the voice was clearer. "Take two paces to your right," it instructed.

Avan glanced at Elric. "What was that?" Elric told him. "Shall we obey?" Avan asked.

"Aye." There was resignation in the albino's voice.

They took two paces to their right.

"Now four to your left," said the voice.

They took four paces to their left.

"Now one forward."

They emerged into the ruined square of R'lin K'ren A'a.

Moonglum and one Vilmirian crewman stood there.

"Where are the others?" Avan demanded.

"Ask him," Moonglum said wearily, gesturing with the sword in his right hand.

They stared at the man who was either an albino or a leper. He was completely naked and he bore a distinct likeness to Elric. At first Elric thought this was another phantom, but then he saw that there were also several differences in their faces. There was something sticking from the man's side, just above the third rib. With a shock Elric recognized it as the broken shaft of a Vilmirian arrow.

The naked man nodded. "Aye—the arrow found its mark. But it could not slay me, for I am J'osui C'reln Reyr. . . ."

"You believe yourself to be the Creature Doomed to Live," Elric murmured.

"I am he." The man gave a bitter smile. "Do you think I try to deceive you?"

Elric glanced at the arrow shaft and then shook his head.

"You are ten thousand years old?" Avan stared at him.

"What does he say?" asked J'osui C'reln Reyr of Elric. Elric translated.

"Is that all it has been?" The man sighed. Then he looked intently at Elric. "You are of my race?"

"It seems so."

"Of what family?"

"Of the Royal line."

"Then you have come at last. I, too, am of that line."

"I believe you."

"I notice that the Olab seek you."

"The Olab?"

"Those primitives with the clubs."

"Aye. We encountered them on our journey up-river."

"I will lead you to safety. Come."

Elric allowed J'osui C'reln Reyr to take them across the square to where part of a tottering wall still stood. The man then lifted a flagstone and showed them the steps leading down into darkness. They followed him, descending cautiously as he caused the flagstone to lower itself above their heads. And then they found themselves in a room lit by crude oil lamps. Save for a bed of dried grasses the room was empty.

"You live sparely," Elric said.

"I have need for nothing else. My head is sufficiently furnished. . . ."

"Where do the Olab come from?" Elric asked.

"They are but recently arrived in these parts. Scarcely a thousand years ago—or perhaps half that time—they came from farther upriver after some quarrel with another tribe. They do not usually come to the island. You must have killed many of them for them to wish you such harm."

"We killed many."

J'osui C'reln Reyr gestured at the others, who were staring at him in some discomfort. "And these? Primitives also, eh? They are not of our folk."

"There are few of our folk left."

"What does he say?" Duke Avan asked.

"He says that those reptile warriors are called the Olab," Elric told him.

"And was it these Olab who stole the Jade Man's eyes?"

As Elric translated the question the Creature Doomed to Live was astonished. "Did you not know, then?"

"Know what?"

"Why, you have been *in* the Jade Man's eyes! Those great crystals in which you wandered—that is what they are!"

7

WHEN ELRIC OFFERED this information to Duke Avan, the Vilmirian burst into laughter. He flung his head back and roared with mirth while the others looked gloomily on. The cloud that had fallen across his features of late suddenly cleared and he became again the man whom Elric had first met in Chalal.

Moonglum was the next to smile, and even Elric acknowledged the irony of what had happened to them.

"Those crystals fell from his face like tears soon after the High Ones departed," continued J'osui C'reln Reyr.

"So the High Ones did come here."

"Aye—the Jade Man brought the message and all the folk departed, having made their bargain with him."

"The Jade Man was not built by your people?"

"The Jade Man is Duke Arioch of Hell. He strode from the forest one day and stood in the square and told the people what was to come about—that our city lay at the center of some particular configuration and that it was only there that the Lords of the Higher Worlds could meet."

"And the bargain?"

"In return for their city our Royal line might in future increase their power, with Arioch as their patron. He would give them great knowledge and the means to build a new city elsewhere."

"And they accepted this bargain without question?"

"There was little choice, kinsman."

Elric lowered his eyes to regard the dusty floor. "And thus they were corrupted," he murmured.

"Only I refuse to accept the pact. I did not wish to leave this city and I mistrusted Arioch. When all others set off down the river, I remained here—where we are now—and I heard the Lords of the Higher Worlds arrive and I heard them speak, laying down the rules under which Law and Chaos would fight thereafter. When they had gone, I emerged. But Arioch—the Jade Man—was still here. He looked down on me through his crystal eyes and he cursed me. When that was done the crystals fell and landed where you now see them. Arioch's spirit departed, but his jade image was left behind."

85

"And you still retain all memory of what transpired between the Lords of Law and Chaos?"

"That is my doom."

"Perhaps your fate was less harsh than that which befell those who left," Elric said quietly. "I am the last inheritor of that particular doom. . . ."

J'osui C'reln Reyr looked puzzled, and then he stared into Elric's eyes and an expession of pity crossed his face. "I had not thought there was a worse fate—but now I believe there might be. . . ."

Elric said urgently, "Ease my soul, at least. I must know what passed between the High Lords in those days. I must understand the nature of my existence—as you, at least, understand yours. Tell me, I beg you!"

J'osui C'reln Reyr frowned and he stared deeply into Elric's eyes. "Do you not know all my story, then?"

"Is there more?"

"I can only *remember* what passed between the High Lords—but when I try to tell my knowledge aloud or try to write it down, I cannot. . . ."

Elric grasped the man's shoulders. "You must try! You must try!"

"I know that I cannot."

Seeing the torture in Elric's face, Moonglum came up to him. "What is it, Elric?"

Elric's hands clutched his head. "Our journey has been useless." Unconciously he used the old Melnibonéan tongue.

"It need not be," said J'osui C'reln Reyr. "For me, at least." He paused. "Tell me, how did you find this city? Was there a map?"

Elric produced the map. "This one."

"Aye, that is the one. Many centuries ago I put it into a casket which I placed in a small trunk. I launched the trunk into the river, hoping that it would follow my people and they would know what it was."

"The casket was found in Melniboné, but no one had bothered

86

to open it," Elric explained. "That will give you an idea of what happened to the folk who left here. . . ."

The strange man nodded gravely. "And was there still a seal upon the map?"

"There was. I have it."

"An image of one of the manifestations of Arioch, imbedded in a small ruby?"

"Aye. I thought I recognized the image, but I could not place it."

"The Image in the Gem," murmured J'osui C'reln Reyr. "As I prayed, it has returned—borne by one of the Royal line!"

"What is its significance?"

Moonglum interrupted. "Will this fellow help us to escape, Elric? We are becoming somewhat impatient. . . ."

"Wait," the albino said. "I will tell you everything later."

"The Image in the Gem could be the instrument of my release," said the Creature Doomed to Live. "If he who possesses it is of the Royal line, then he can command the Jade Man."

"But why did you not use it?"

"Because of the curse that was put on me. I had the power to command but not to summon the demon. It was a joke, I understand, of the High Lords."

Elric saw bitter sadness in the eyes of J'osui C'reln Reyr. He looked at the white, naked flesh and the white hair and the body that was neither old nor young, at the shaft of the arrow sticking out above the third rib on the left side.

"What must I do?" he asked.

"You must summon Arioch and then you must command him to enter his body again and recover his eyes so that he may see to walk away from R'lin K'ren A'a."

"And when he walks away?"

"The curse goes with him."

Elric was thoughtful. If he did summon Arioch—who was plainly reluctant to come—and then commanded him to do something he did not wish to do, he stood the chance of making an enemy of that

87

powerful, if unpredictable, entity. Yet they were trapped here by the Olab warriors, with no means of escaping them. If the Jade Man walked, the Olab would almost certainly flee, and there would be time to get back to the ship and reach the sea. He explained everything to his companions. Both Moonglum and Avan looked dubious and the remaining Vilmirian crewman looked positively terrified.

"I must do it," Elric decided, "for the sake of this man. I must call Arioch and lift the doom that is on R'lin K'ren A'a."

"And bring a greater doom to us!" Duke Avan said, putting his hand automatically upon his sword hilt. "No. I think we should take our chances with the Olab. Leave this man—he is mad—he raves. Let's be on our way."

"Go if you choose," Elric said. "But I will stay with the Creature Doomed to Live."

"Then you will stay here forever. You cannot believe his story!"

"But I do believe it."

"You must come with us. Your sword will help. Without it, the Olab will certainly destroy us."

"You saw that Stormbringer has little effect against the Olab."

"And yet it has some. Do not desert me, Elric!"

"I am not deserting you. I must summon Arioch. That summoning will be to your benefit, if not to mine."

"I am unconvinced."

"It was my sorcery you wanted on this venture. Now you shall have my sorcery."

Avan backed away. He seemed to fear more than the Olab, more than the summoning. He seemed to read something in Elric's face which even Elric did not know.

"We must go outside," said J'osui C'reln Reyr. "We must stand beneath the Jade Man."

"And when this is done," Elric asked suddenly, "how could we leave R'lin K'ren A'a?"

"There is a boat. It has no provisions, but much of the city's treasure is on it. It lies at the west end of the island."

"That is some comfort," Elric said. "And you could not use it yourself?"

"I could not leave."

"Is that part of the curse?"

"Aye—the curse of my timidity."

"Timidity has kept you here ten thousand years?"

"Aye . . ."

They left the chamber and went out into the square. Night had fallen and a huge moon was in the sky. From where Elric stood it seemed to frame the Jade Man's sightless head like a halo. It was completely silent. Elric took the Image in the Gem from his pouch and held it between the forefinger and thumb of his left hand. With his right he drew Stormbringer. Avan, Moonglum and the Vilmirian crewman fell back.

He stared up at the huge jade legs, the genitals, the torso, the arms, the head, and he raised his sword in both hands and screamed:

"ARIOCH!"

Stormbringer's voice almost drowned his. It pulsed in his hands, it threatened to leave his grasp altogether as it howled.

"ARIOCH!"

All the watchers saw now was the throbbing, radiant sword, the white face and hands of the albino and his crimson eyes glaring through the blackness.

"ARIOCH!"

And then a voice which was not Arioch's came to Elric's ears, and it seemed that the sword itself spoke.

"Elric—Arioch must have blood and souls. Blood and souls, my lord."

"No. These are my friends and the Olab cannot be harmed by Stormbringer. Arioch must come without the blood, without the souls."

"Only those can summon him for certain!" said a voice, more

clearly now. It was sardonic and it seemed to come from behind him. He turned, but there was nothing there.

He saw Duke Avan's nervous face and, as his eyes fixed on the Vilmirian's countenance, the sword came round and plunged toward the duke.

"No!" cried Elric. "Stop!"

But Stormbringer would not stop until it had bitten deep into Duke Avan's heart and quenched its thirst. The crewman stood transfixed as he watched his master die.

Duke Avan writhed. "Elric! What treachery do you . . . ?" He screamed. "Ah, no!"

He jerked. "Please . . ."

He quivered. "My soul . . ."

He died.

Elric withdrew the sword and cut the crewman down. The action had been without thought.

"Now Arioch has his blood and his souls," he said coldly. "Let Arioch come!"

Moonglum and the Creature Doomed to Live had retreated, staring at the possessed Elric in horror. The albino's face was cruel.

"LET ARIOCH COME!"

"I am here, Elric."

Elric whirled and saw that something stood in the shadow of the statue's legs—a shadow within a shadow.

"Arioch—thou must return to this manifestation and make it leave R'lin K'ren A'a forever."

"I do not choose to, Elric."

"Then I must command thee, Duke Arioch."

"Command? Only he who possesses the Image in the Gem may command Arioch—and then only once."

"I have the Image in the Gem." Elric held the tiny object up. "See!"

The shadow within a shadow swirled for a moment as if in anger.

"If I obey your command, you will set in motion a chain of events which you might not desire," Arioch said, speaking suddenly in Low Melnibonéan, as if to give extra gravity to his words.

"Then let it be. I command you to enter the Jade Man and pick up its eyes so that it might walk again. Then I command you to leave here and take the curse of the High Ones with you."

Arioch replied, "When the Jade Man ceases to guard the place where the High Ones meet, then the great struggle of the Upper Worlds begins."

"I command thee, Arioch. Go into the Jade Man!"

"You are an obstinate creature, Elric."

"Go!" Elric raised Stormbringer. It seemed to sing in monstrous glee, and it seemed at that moment to be more powerful than Arioch himself, more powerful than all the Lords of the Higher Worlds.

The ground shook. Fire suddenly blazed around the form of the great statue. The shadow within a shadow disappeared.

And the Jade Man stooped.

Its great bulk bent over Elric and its hands reached past him and it groped for the two crystals that lay on the ground. Then it found them and took one in each hand, straightening its back.

Elric stumbled toward the far corner of the square, where Moonglum and J'osui C'reln Reyr already stood, their bodies crouched in terror.

A fierce light now blazed from the Jade Man's eyes and the jade lips parted.

"It is done, Elric!" said a huge voice.

J'osui C'reln Reyr began to sob.

"Then go, Arioch."

"I go. The curse is lifted from R'lin K'ren A'a and from J'osui C'reln Reyr—but a greater curse now lies upon your whole plane. I journey now to Pan Tang to answer, at last, the Theocrat's prayers to me!"

"What is this, Arioch? Explain yourself!" Elric cried.

"Soon you will have your explanation. Farewell!"

The enormous legs of jade moved suddenly and in a single step had cleared the ruins and had begun to crash through the jungle. In a moment the Jade Man had disappeared.

Then the Creature Doomed to Live laughed. It was a strange joy that he voiced. Moonglum blocked his ears.

"And now!" shouted J'osui C'reln Reyr. "Now your blade must take my life. I can die at last!"

Elric passed his hand across his face. He had hardly been aware of the events of the past moments. "No," he said in a dazed tone. "I cannot . . ."

And Stormbringer flew from his hand—flew to the body of the Creature Doomed to Live and buried itself in its chest.

And as he died, J'osui C'reln Reyr laughed. He fell to the ground and his lips moved. A whisper came from them. Elric stepped nearer to hear.

"The sword has my knowledge now. My burden has left me."

The eyes closed.

J'osui C'reln Reyr's ten-thousand-year life span had ended.

Weakly Elric withdrew Stormbringer and sheathed it. He stared down at the body of the Creature Doomed to Live and then he looked up, questioningly, at Moonglum.

The little Eastlander turned away.

The sun began to rise. Gray dawn came. Elric watched the corpse of J'osui C'reln Reyr turn to powder that was stirred by the wind and mixed with the dust of the ruins. He walked back across the square to where Duke Avan's twisted body lay and he fell to his knees beside it.

"You were warned, Duke Avan Astran of Old Hrolmar, that ill befell those who linked their fortunes with Elric of Melniboné. But you thought otherwise. Now you know." With a sigh he got to his feet.

Moonglum stood beside him. The sun was touching the taller parts of the ruins. Moonglum reached out and gripped his friend's shoulder.

"The Olab have vanished. I think they've had their fill of sorcery."

"Another one has been destroyed by me, Moonglum. Must I forever be tied to this cursed sword? I must discover a way to rid myself of it or my heavy conscience will bear me down so that I cannot rise at all."

Moonglum nodded but was silent.

"I will lay Duke Avan to rest," Elric said. "You go back to where we left the ship and tell the men that we come."

Moonglum began to walk across the square toward the east.

Elric tenderly picked up the body of Duke Avan and went toward the opposite side of the square, to the underground room where the Creature Doomed to Live had lived out his life for ten thousand years.

It seemed so unreal to Elric now, but he knew that it had not been a dream, for the Jade Man had gone. His tracks could be seen through the jungle. Whole clumps of trees had been flattened.

He reached the place and descended the stairs and laid Duke Avan down on the bed of dried grasses. Then he took the duke's dagger and, for want of anything else, dipped it in the duke's blood and wrote on the wall above the corpse:

This was Duke Avan Astran of Old Hrolmar. He explored the world and brought much knowledge and treasure back to Vilmir, his land. He dreamed and became lost in the dream of another, and so died. He enriched the Young Kingdoms—and thus encouraged another dream. He died so that the Creature Doomed to Live might die, as he desired.

Elric paused. Then he threw down the dagger. He could not justify his own feelings of guilt by composing a high-sounding epitaph for the man he had slain.

He stood there, breathing heavily, then once again picked up the dagger.

He died because Elric of Melniboné desired a peace and a knowledge he could never find. He died by the Black Sword.

93

Outside in the middle of the square at noon still lay the lonely body of the last Vilmirian crewman. Nobody had known his name. Nobody felt grief for him or tried to compose an epitaph for him. The dead Vilmirian had died for no high purpose, followed no fabulous dream. Even in death his body would fulfill no function. On this island there was no carrion to feed. In the dust of the city there was no earth to fertilize.

Elric came back into the square and saw the body, and for him, for a moment, it symbolized everything that had transpired here and would transpire later.

"There is no purpose," he murmured.

Perhaps his remote ancestors had, after all, realized that, but had not cared. It had taken the Jade Man to make them care and then go mad in their anguish. The knowledge had caused them to close their minds to much.

"Elric!"

It was Moonglum returning. Elric looked up.

"The Olab dealt with the crew and the ship before they came after us. They're all slain. The boat is destroyed."

Elric remembered something the Creature Doomed to Live had told him. "There is another boat," he said. "On the west side of the island."

It took them the rest of the day and that night to discover where J'osui C'reln Reyr had hidden his boat. They pulled it down to the water and inspected it. It was a sturdy boat, made of the same strange material they had seen in the library of R'lin K'ren A'a. Moonglum peered into the lockers and grinned at what he saw there. "Treasure! So we have benefited from this venture, after all!"

"The jewels will not feed us," Elric said. "It is a long journey home."

"Home?"

"Back to the Young Kingdoms."

Moonglum winked at him. "I saw some cases of provisions

amongst the wreckage of Avan's schooner. We'll sail around the island and pick them up."

Elric looked back at the silent forest and a shiver passed through him. He thought of all the hopes he had had on the journey up-river and he cursed himself for a fool.

There was something of a smile on his face as they cast off, hoisted the sail and began to move with the current.

Moonglum displayed a handful of emeralds. "We are poor no longer, friend Elric!"

"Aye," said Elric. "Are we not lucky, you and I, Moonglum?"

And this time it was Moonglum's turn to shiver.

It is no secret that the enormously prolific and popular author of fifty or sixty teen-age science fiction adventure novels who writes under the pseudonym of Andre Norton is really a former children's librarian from Cleveland, Ohio, whose real name is Alice Mary Norton.

Miss Norton has now retired and moved to Maitland, Florida, where she is busily at work on her next fifty or sixty enormously popular teen-age science fiction adventure novels.

In person she is a gray-haired, sweetly smiling, fiftyish woman of tremendous energy and enthusiasm. Her first novel, an adventure story entitled *The Prince Commands*, was published by Appleton, Century, Crofts in 1934. She has written lots of other stuff besides science fiction, including juvenile fantasy novels, historicals, westerns, pirate yarns, Civil War stories and at least one murder mystery. While by far the bulk of her work has been in the area of fast-paced, colorful space adventure stories for young readers, she merits a place in SAGA for an unusual sequence of (thus far) six novels which began with *Witch World* (1963) and continued with *Web of the Witch World* (1964), *Three Against the Witch World* (1965), *Year of the Unicorn* (also 1965), *Warlock of the Witch World* (1967) and, most recently, *Sorceress of the Witch World* (1968), all published by Ace Books.

While I have nothing against her science fiction juveniles, I must admit that to my personal taste these "Witch World" books seem far and away her best. They are mature works of sensitive craftsmanship, written with slower pace and richer background detail and more adult character development than I have found in her other novels. Unfortunately the series seems to have ended: at least we have had no new "Witch World" story from her hand for three years now.

The acceptance by Dell Books of this two-volume SAGA anthology prompted me to write Miss Norton (our only Swordswoman & Sorceress, by the way), asking for a new story— preferably a Witch World tale. She replied with alacrity that she would be delighted to return to Witch World for at least one more story, and the result follows next.

Toads of Grimmerdale

by ANDRE NORTON

THE DRIFTS of ice-crusted snow were growing both taller and wider. Hertha stopped to catch her breath, ramming the butt of the hunting spear she had been using as a staff into the drift before her, the smooth shaft breaking through the crust with difficulty. She frowned at the broken hole without seeing it.

There was a long dagger at her belt, the short-hafted spear in her mittened hand. And under her cloak she hugged to her the all too small bundle which she had brought with her out of Horla's Hold. The other burden which she carried lay within her, and she forced herself to face squarely the fate it had brought upon her.

Now her lips firmed into a line, her chin went up. Suddenly she spat with a hiss of breath. Shame—why should she feel shame? Had Kuno expected her to whine and wail, perhaps crawl before him so he could "forgive" her, prove thus to his followers his greatness of spirit?

She showed her teeth as might a cornered vixen and aimed a harder blow at the drift. There was no reason for her to feel shame, the burden in her was not of wanton seeking. Such things happened in times of war. She guessed that when matters worked so, Kuno had not been backward himself in taking a woman of the enemy.

It remained that her noble brother had sent her forth from Horla's Hold because she had not allowed his kitchen hags to brew some foul potion to perhaps poison her, as well as what she bore. Had she so died he could have piously crossed hands at the Thunderer's altar and spoken of Fate's will. And it would have ended neatly. In fact she might believe that perhaps that had been the intention.

For a moment Hertha was startled at the grim march of her thoughts. Kuno—Kuno was her *brother!* Two years ago she could not have thought so of him or any man! Before the war nearer the Hold. But that was long before she set out for Landendale. Before she knew the world as it was and not as she had believed it.

Hertha was glad she had been able to learn her lesson quickly. The thin-skinned maid she had once been could not have fronted Kuno, could not have taken this road—

She felt the warmth of anger, a sullen, glowing anger, heating as if she carried a small brazier of coals under her cloak's edge. So she went on, setting her rough boots firmly to crunch across the drift edge. Nor did she turn to look back down at that stone walled keep which had sheltered those of her blood for five generations. The sun was well westward, she must not linger on the trail. Few paths were broken now, times in number she must halt and use the spear to sound out the footing. But it was easy to keep in eye her landmarks of Mulma's Needle and the Wyvern's Wing.

Hertha was sure Kuno expected her to return to accept his conditions. She smiled wryly. Kuno was so very certain of everything. And since he had beaten off the attack of a straggling band of the enemy trying to fight their way to the dubious safety of the coast, he had been insufferable.

The Dales were free in truth. But for Kuno to act as if the victories hard won there were his alone—! It had required all the might of High Hallack, together with strange allies from the Waste, to break the invaders, to hunt and harry them to the sea from which they had come. And that had taken a score of years to do.

Trewsdale had escaped, not because of any virtue, but by chance. But because fire and sword had not riven there was no reason to cry upon unbroken walls like gamecocks. Kuno had harried men already three-quarters beaten.

She reached the divide, to plod steadily on. The wind had been at work here, and her path was free of snow. It was very old, that road, one of the reminders to be found all across the dale land that her own people were late comers. Who had cut these ways for their own treading?

The well-weathered carvings at the foot of the Wyvern's Wing could be seen easily now. So eroded they were by time that none could trace their meaning. But men—or intelligent beings—had shaped them to a purpose. And that task must have been long in the doing. Hertha reached out her mittened fingers to mark one of the now vague curves. She did not believe they had any virtue in themselves, though the field workers did. But they marked well her road.

Downslope again from this point, and now the wind's lash did not cut at her. Though again snow drifted. Two tens of days yet to the feast of Year Turn. This was the last of the Year of the Hornet, next lay the Year of the Unicorn, which was a more fortunate sign.

With the increase of snow Hertha once more found the footing dangerous. The bits of broken crust worked in over the tops of her boots, even though she had drawn tight their top straps, melted clammily against her foot sacks. She plodded on as the track entered a fringe of scrub trees.

Evergreens, the foliage was dark in the dwindling light. But they arose to roof over a road, keep off the drifts. And she came to a stream where ice had bridged from one stony bank to the other. There she turned east to gain Gunnora's shrine.

About its walls was a tangle of winter-killed garden. It was a low building, and an archway faced her. No gate or door barred that and she walked boldly in.

Once inside the outer wall she could see windows—round like the eyes of some great feline regarding her sleepily—flanking a door by which hung a heavy bell-pull of wrought metal in the form of Gunnora's symbol of a ripened grain stalk entwined with a fruit-laden branch.

Hertha leaned her spear against the wall that her hand might be free for a summons pull. What answered was not any peal of bell, rather an odd, muted sound, as if some one called in words she did not understand. That, too, she accepted, though she had not been this way before and had only a few whispered words to send her here.

The leaves of the door parted. Though no one stood there to give her house greeting, Hertha took that for an invitation to enter. She moved into gentle warmth, a fragrance of herbs and flowers. As if she had, in that single step, passed from the sere death of midwinter into the life of spring.

With the warmth and fragrance came a lightening of heart, so that the taut lines in her face smoothed a little and her aching shoulders and back lost some of the stiffening tension.

What light there was came from two lamps set on columns, one right, one left. She was in a narrow entry, its walls painted with such colors as to make her believe that she had truly entered a garden. Before her those ranks of flowers rippled, and she realized that there hung a curtain, fashioned to repeat the wall design. Since there still came no greeting, she put out her hand to the folds of that curtain.

But before she could finger it the length looped aside of itself, and she came into a large room. Inside was a table with a chair drawn up to it. The table was set with dishes, some covered as if they held viands which were to be kept warm, and a goblet of crystal filled with a green liquid.

"Eat—drink—" a voice sighed through the chamber.

Startled, Hertha looked about the room over her shoulder. No one— And now that hunger of which she had hardly been aware awoke full force. She dropped the spear to the floor, laid her bundle beside it, let her cloak fall over both, and sat down in the chair.

Though she could see no one, she spoke:

"To the giver of the feast, fair thanks. For the welcome of the gate, gratitude. To the ruler of this house, fair fortune and bright sun on the morrow—" The formal words rang a little hollow here. Hertha smiled at a sudden thought.

This was Gunnora's shrine. Would the Great Lady need the well-wishing of any mortal? Yet it seemed fitting that she make the guest speech.

There was no answer, though she hoped for one. At last, a little hesitantly, she sampled the food spread before her, and found it such fare as might be on the feast table of a Dales Lord. The green drink was refreshing, yet warming, with a subtle taste of herbs. She held it in her mouth, trying to guess which gave it that flavor.

When she had finished she found that the last and largest covered basin held warm water, on the surface of which floated petals of flowers. Flowers in the dead of winter! And beside it was a towel, so she washed her hands and leaned back in the chair, wondering what came next in Gunnora's hall.

The silence in the room seemed to grow the greater. Hertha stirred. Surely there were priestesses at the Shrine? Some one had prepared that meal, offered it to her with those two words. She had come here for a purpose, and the need for action roused in her again.

"Great Lady," Hertha arose. Since she could see no one, she would speak to the empty room. There was a door at the other end of the chamber, but it was closed.

"Great Lady," she began again. She had never been deeply religious, though she kept Light Day, made the harvest sacrifices, listened respectfully to the Mouth of Astron at Morn Service. When she had been a little maid her foster mother had given her Gunnora's apple as a pendant to wear. But according to custom that had been laid on the house altar when she came to marriageable age. Of Gunnora's mysteries she knew only what she had heard repeated woman to woman when they sat apart from the men. For Gunnora was only for womankind, and when one was carrying ripening seed within one, then she listened—

For the second time her words echoed. Now that feeling of impatience changed to something else—awe, perhaps, or fear? Yet Gunnora did not hold by the petty rules of men. It did not matter when you sought her if you be lawful wife or not.

As her distrust grew the second door swung silently open—another invitation. Leaving her cloak, bundle, spear where they lay, Hertha went on. Here the smell of flowers and herbs was stronger. Lazy curls of scented smoke arose from two braziers standing at the head and foot of a couch, set as an altar at the foot of a pillar carved with the ripened grain and fruited branch.

"Rest—" the sighing voice bade. And Hertha, the need for sleep suddenly as great as her hunger had been, moved to that waiting bed, stretched out her wearied and aching body. The curls of smoke thickened, spread over her as a coverlet. She closed her eyes.

She was in a place of half light in which she sensed others coming and going, busied about tasks. But she felt alone, lost. Then one moved to her and she saw a face she knew, though a barrier of years had half dimmed it in her mind.

"Elfreda!" Hertha believed she had not called that name aloud,

104

only thought it. But her foster mother smiled, holding out her arms in the old, old welcome.

"Little dove, little love—" The old words were as soothing as healing salve laid on an angry wound.

Years came as Hertha had not allowed them to come before. She wept out sore hurt and was comforted. Then that shade who was Elfreda drew her on, past all those about their work, into a place of light, in which there was Another. And that one Hertha could not look upon directly. But she heard a question asked, and to it she made truthful answer.

"No," she pressed her hands to her body, "what I carry I do not want to lose."

And that brightness which was the Other grew. But there was another question, and again Hertha answered:

"I hold two desires—that this child be mine alone, taking of no other heritage from the manner of its begetting and him who forced me so. And, second, I wish to bring to account the one who will not stand as its father."

There was a long moment before the reply came. Then a spear of light shot from the center core of the radiance, traced a symbol before Hertha. Though she had no training in the Mysteries yet, this was plain for her reading.

Her first prayer would be answered. The coming child would be only of her, taking naught from her ravisher. And the destiny for it was auspicious. But, though she waited, there was no second answer. The great One—was gone! But Elfreda was still with her, and Hertha turned to her quickly:

"What of my need for justice?"

"Vengeance is not of the Lady." Elfreda shook her veiled head. "She is life, not death. Since you have chosen to give life, she will aid you in that. For the rest—you must walk another road. But— do not take it, my love—for out of darkness comes even greater dark."

Then Hertha lost Elfreda also and there was nothing, only the memory of what happened in that place. So she fell into deeper slumber where no dreams walked.

She awoke, how much later she never knew. But she was renewed in mind and body, feeling as if some leechcraft had been at work during her rest, banishing all ills. There was no more smoke rising from the braziers, the scent of flowers was faint.

When she arose from the couch she knelt before the pillar, bowing her head, giving thanks. Yet still in her worked her second desire, in nowise lessened by Elfreda's warning.

In the outer room there was again food and drink waiting. And she ate and drank before she went forth from Gunnora's house. There was no kin far or near she might take refuge with. Kuno had made loud her shame when he sent her forth. She had a few bits of jewelry, none of worth, sewn into her girdle, some pieces of trade money. Beyond that she had only a housewife's skills, and those not of the common sort, rather the distilling of herbs, the making of ointments, the fine sewing of a lady's teaching. She could read, write, sing a stave—none of these arts conducive to the earning of one's bread.

Yet her spirit refused to be darkened by hard facts. From her waking that sense of things about to come right held. And she thought it best that she limit the future to one day ahead at a time.

In the direction she now faced lay two holdings. Nordendale was the first. It was small and perhaps in a state of disorder. The lord of the dale and his heir had both fallen at the battle of Ruther's Pass, two years gone. Who kept order there now, if there was any who ruled, she did not know. Beyond that lay Grimmerdale.

Grimmerdale! Hertha set down the goblet from which she had drained the last drop. Grimmerdale—

Just as the shrine of Gunnora was among the heights near the ancient road, so did Grimmerdale have a place of mystery. But no kind and welcoming one if rumor spoke true. Not of her race at all, but one as old as the ridge road. In fact perhaps that road had first been cut to run there.

Hertha tried to recall all she had heard of Grimmerdale. Somewhere in the heights there was the Circle of the Toads. Men had gone there, asked for certain things. By ill report they had received all they asked for. What had Elfreda warned—that Gunnora did not grant death, that one must follow another path to find that. Grimmerdale might be the answer.

She looked about her, almost in challenge, half expecting to feel condemnation in the air of the room. But there was nothing.

"For the feast, my thanks," she spoke the guesting words, "for the roof, my blessing, for the future all good, as I take my road again."

She fastened the throat latch of her cloak, drew the hood over her head. Then with bundle in one hand and spear in the other, she went out into the light of day, her face to the ridges behind which lay Grimmerdale.

On the final slope above Nordendale she paused in the afternoon to study the small settlement below. It was inhabited, there was a curl of smoke from more than one chimney, the marks of sleds, foot prints in the snow. But the tower keep showed no such signs of life.

How far ahead still lay Grimmerdale she did not know, and night came early in the winter. One of those cottages below was larger than the rest. Nordendale had once been a regular halt for herdsmen with wool from mountain sheep on their way to the market at Komm High. That market was of the past, but the inn might still abide, at least be willing to give her shelter.

She was breathing hard when she trudged into the slush of the road below. But she had been right, over the door of the largest cottage hung a wind-battered board, its painted device long weathered away but still proclaiming this an inn. She made for that, passing a couple of men on the way. They stared at her as if she were a fire-drake or wyvern. Strangers must be few in Nordendale.

The smell of food, sour village ale, and too many people too long in an unaired space was like a smothering fog as she came into the common room. At one end was a wide hearth, large enough to take a good-sized log, and fire burned there, giving off a goodly heat.

A trestle table with flanking benches, and a smaller table stacked with tankards and settles by the hearth were the only furnishings. As Hertha entered, a wench in a stained smock and kirtle and two men on a hearth settle, turned and started with the same astonishment she had seen without.

She pushed back her hood and looked back at them with that belief in herself which was her heritage.

"Good fortune to this house."

For a moment they made no answer at all, seemingly too taken back at seeing a stranger to speak. Then the maidservant came forward, wiping her hands on her already well besplattered apron.

"Good fortune"— Her eyes were busy taking in the fine material of Hertha's cloak, her air of ease—"lady. How may we serve you?"

"With food, a bed—if such you have."

"Food—food we have, but it be plain, coarse feeding, lady," the girl stammered. "Let me but call mistress—"

She ran to an inner door, bolting through it as if Hertha was minded to pursue her.

But she rather laid aside her spear and bundle, threw back the edges of her cloak and went to stand before the hearth, pulling with her teeth at mitten fastenings, to bare her chilled hands. The men hunched away along the settle, mum-mouthed and still staring.

Hertha had thought her clothing plain. She wore one of the divided riding skirts, cut shorter for the scrambling up and down of hills, and it was now shabby and much worn, yet very serviceable. There was an embroidered edge on her jerkin, but no wider than some farm daughter might have. And her hair was tight braided, with no band of ribbon or silver to hold it so. Yet she might be clad in some festival finery the way they looked upon her. And she stood as impassive as she could under their stares.

A woman wearing the close coif of a matron, a loose shawl about her bent shoulders, a kirtle but little cleaner than the maid's, looped up about her wide hips and thick thighs, bustled in.

"Welcome, my lady. Thrice welcome! Up you, Henkin, Sim, let the lady to the fire!" The men pushed away in a hurry at her ordering. "Malka says you would bide the night. This roof is honored."

"I give thanks."

"Your man—outside? We have stabling—"

Hertha shook her head. "I journey alone and on foot." At the look on the woman's face she added, "In these days we take what fortune offers, we do not always please ourselves."

"Alas, lady, that is true speaking if such ever came to ear! Sit you down!" She jerked off her shawl and used it to dust along the settle.

Later, in a bed spread with coverings fire warmed, in a room which manifestly had been shut up for some time, Hertha lay in what comfort such a place could offer and mused over what she had learned from her hostess.

As she had heard, Nordendale had fallen on dreary times. Along with their lord and his heir, most of their able bodied men had been slain. Those who survived and drifted back lacked leadership and had done little to restore what had been a prosperous village. There were very few travelers along the road, she had been the first since winter closed in. Things were supposed to be somewhat better in the east and south and her tale of going to kinsmen there had seemed plausible to those below.

Better still she had news of Grimmerdale. There was another inn there, a larger place, with more patronage, which the mistress here spoke of wistfully. An east-west road, now seeing much travel with levies going home, ran there. But the innkeeper had a wife who could not keep serving-maids, being of jealous nature.

Of the Toads she dared not ask, and no one had volunteered such information, save that the mistress here had warned against the taking farther of the Old Road, saying it was better to keep to the highway. Though she admitted that was also dangerous and it was well to be ready to take to the brush at the sighting of some travelers.

As yet Hertha had no more than the faint stirrings of a plan. But she was content to wait before she shaped it more firmly.

2

THE INN ROOM was long but low, the crossbeams of its ceiling not far above the crown of a tall man's head. Smoking oil lamps hung on chains from those beams. But the light they gave was both murky and limited. Only at the far corner, where a carven screen afforded some privacy, were there tallow candles set out on a table. And the odor of their burning added to the general smell of the room.

The room was crowded enough to loosen the thin-lipped mouth of Uletka Rory, whose small eyes darted hither and yon, missing no detail of service or lack of service as her two laboring slaves limped and scuttled between benches and stools. She herself waited upon the candlelit table, a mark of favor. She knew high blood when she saw it.

Not that in this case she was altogether right, in spite of her years of dealing with travelers. One of the men there, yes, was the younger son of a dale lord. But his family holding had long since vanished in the red tide of war, and no one was left in Corriedale to name him master. One had been Master of Archers for another lord, promoted hurriedly after three better men had been killed. And the third, well, he was not one who talked, and neither of his present companions knew his past.

Of the three he was the middle in age. Though that, too, could not be easily guessed, since he was one of those lean, spare-framed men who once they begin to sprout beard hair can be any age from youth to middle years. Not that he went bearded now—his chin and jaw were as smooth as if he had scraped them within the hour, displaying along the jaw line the seam of a scar that drew a little at one corner of his lip.

He wore his hair cropped closer than most also, perhaps because of the heavy helm now planted on the table at his right hand. That was battered enough to have served through the war. And the crest it had once mounted was splintered down to a meaningless knob, though the protective bowl was unbreached.

His mail shirt, under a scuffed and worn tabbard, was whole. And the plain hilted sword in his belt sheath, the war bow now resting against the wall at his back were the well-kept tools of a professional. But if he was a mercenary he had not been successful lately. He wore none of those fine buckles or studs which could be easily snapped off to pay for food or lodging. Only when he put out his hand to take up his tankard did the candlelight glint on something which was not dull steel or leather. For the bowguard on his wrist was true treasure, a wide band of cunningly wrought gold set with small colored stones, though the pattern of that design was so complicated that to make anything of it required close study.

He sat now sober-faced, as if he were deep in thought, his eyes half-veiled by heavy lids. But he was in truth listening, not so much to the half drunken mumblings of his companions, but to words arising here and there in the common room.

Most of those gathered there were either workers on the land come in to nurse an earthen mug of home-brewed barley beer and exchange grumbles with their fellows, or else drifting men-at-arms seeking employment now that their lords were dead or so ruined that they had to release the men of their levies. The war was over, these were the victors. But the land they returned to was barren, largely devastated, and it would take much time and energy to win back prosperity for High Hallack.

What the invaders from overseas had not early raped, looted for shiploads sent back to their own lands, they had destroyed in a frenzy when the tide of war began to wash them away. He had been with the war bands in the smoking port, sent to mop up desperate enemies who had fallen back too late to find that their companions had taken off in the last ships, leaving them to be ground between the men of the dales and the sullen sea itself.

The smoke of the port had risen from piles of supplies set burning, oil poured over them and torches set to the spoilage. The stench of it had been near enough to kill a man. Having stripped the country bare—and this being the midwinter—the enemy had made a last defiant gesture with that great fire. It would be a long cold line of days before the coming of summer, and even then men would go pinched of belly until harvest time—harvest if, that is, they could find enough grain to plant, if enough sheep still roamed the upper dales and enough cattle, wild now, found forage in the edges of the Waste to make a beginning of new flocks and herds.

Many dales had been swept clean of people. The men were dead in battle; the women were fled inland, if they were lucky, or slaving for the invaders overseas—or dead also. Perhaps those were the luckiest of all. Yes, there had been a great shaking and leveling, sorting and spilling.

He had put down the tankard. Now his other hand went to that bowguard, turning it about, though he did not look down at it, but rather stared at the screen and listened.

In such a time a man with boldness, and a plan, could begin a new life. That was what had brought him inland, kept him from taking service with Fritigen of Summersdale. Who would be Master of Archers when he could be more, much more?

The invaders had not reached this Grimmerdale, but there were other lands beyond with darker luck. He was going to find one of those—one where there was no lord left to sound the war horn. If there was a lady trying to hold a heritage, well, that might even fit well with his ambitions. Now his tongue showed for an instant on his lower lip, flicking across as if he savored in anticipation some dish which pleased him. He did not altogether believe in the override of good or ill fortune. In his calculations a man mostly made his own luck by knowing what he wanted and bending all his actions toward that end. But he had a feeling that this was the time when he must move if he were ever to bring to truth the dream which had lain in him since early boyhood.

He, Trystan out of nowhere, was going to end Lord Trystan of some not inconsiderable stretch of land—with a keep for his home and a dale under his rule. And the time to move was here and now.

"Fill!" His near companion, young Urre, pounded his tankard on the table top so that one of the candles shook, spattering hot grease. He bellowed an oath and threw his empty pot beyond the screen to clatter across the flagstones.

The lame pot boy stooped to pick it up, casting a frightened look at Urre and a second at his scowling mistress, who was already on her way with a tray of freshly-filled tankards. Trystan pushed back from the table. They were following a path he had seen too many nights. Urre would drink himself sodden, sick not only with the rank stuff they called drink back here in the hills, but also with his life, wherein he could only bewail what he had lost, taking no thought of what might be gained.

Onsway would listen attentively to his mumbling, willing to play liegeman as long as Urre's money lasted, or he could use his kin ties to win them food and lodging at some keep. When Urre made a final sot of himself, Onsway would no longer wallow in the sty beside him. While he, Trystan, thought it time now to cut the thread which had brought them this far in uneasy company. Neither had anything to give, and he knew now that traveling longer with them he would not do.

But he was not minded to quit this inn soon. Its position on the highway was such that a man could pick up a wealth of information by just sitting and listening. Also, here he had already picked out two likely prospects for his own purposes. The money pouch at his belt was flat enough, he could not afford to spin a coin before the dazzled eyes of an archer or pike man and offer employment.

However, there were men like himself to be found, rootless men who wanted roots in better circumstances than they had known, men who could see the advantage of service under a rising man with opportunities for rising themselves in his wake. One did not need a large war band to overawe masterless peasants; half a dozen well-armed and experienced fighting men at his back, a dale without a lord—and he would be in!

Excitement awoke in him as it did every time his plan reached that place in his thoughts. But he had learned long since to keep a tight rein on his emotions. He was a controlled man, abstemious to a degree astounding among his fellows, though he did what he could to conceal that difference. He could loot, he could whore, he could kill—and he had—but always calculatingly.

"I'm for bed," he arose and reached for his bow, "the road this day was long—"

Urre might not have heard him at all, his attention was fixed on the tray of tankards. Onsway nodded absently; he was watching Urre as he always did. But the mistress was alert to the hint of more profit.

"Bed, good master? Three coins—and a fire on the hearth, too."

"Good enough." He nodded, and she screeched for the pot boy, who came at a limping waddle, wiping his grimed hands on the black rags of an apron knotted about him.

While the inn gave the impression of space below, on the second floor it was much more cramped. At least the room into which Trystan tramped was no more than a narrow slit of space with a single window covered by a shutter heavily barred. There was a litter of dried rushes on the floor and a rough bed frame, on which a pile of bedding lay as if tossed. The hearth fire promised did not exist. But a legged brazier with some glowing coals gave off a little heat, and a stool beside a warp-sided chest did service as a table. The pot boy set the candle down on that and was ready to scuttle away when Trystan, who had gone to the window, hailed him.

"What manner of siege have you had here, boy? This shutter has been so long barred it is rusted tight."

The boy cringed back against the edge of the door, his slack mouth hanging open. He was an ugly lout, and looked half-witted into the bargain, Trystan thought. But surely there was something more than just stupidity in his face when he looked to the window —there was surely fear also.

"Thhheee tooods—" His speech was thick. He had lifted his hands breast high, was clasping them so tightly together that his knuckles stood out as bony knobs.

Trystan had heard the enemy called many things, but never toads, nor had he believed they had raided into Grimmerdale.

"Toads?" He made a question of the word.

The boy turned his head away so that he looked neither to the window nor at Trystan. It was very evident he planned escape. The man crossed the narrow room with effortless and noiseless strides, caught him by the shoulder.

"What manner of toads?" He shook the boy slightly.

"Toodss—Thhheee toods—" the boy seemed to think Trystan should know of what he spoke. "They—that sit 'mong the Standing Stones—that what do men evil." His voice, while thick, no longer sputtered so. "All men know the Toods o' Grimmerdale!" Then, with a twist which showed he had long experience in escaping, he broke from Trystan's hold and was gone. The man did not pursue him.

Rather he stood frowning in the light of the single candle. Toads —and Grimmerdale—together they had a faintly familiar sound. Now he set memory to work. Toads and Grimmerdale—what did he know of either?

The dale was of importance, more so now than in the days before the war when men favored a more southern route to the port. That highway had fallen almost at once into invader hands, and they had kept it forted and patroled. The answer had been this secondary road, which heretofore had been used mainly by shepherds and herdsmen. Three different trails from upcountry united at the western mouth of Grimmerdale.

However: had he not once heard of yet a fourth way, one which ran the ridges yet was mainly shunned, a very old way, antedating the coming of his own people? Now—he nodded as memory supplied answers. The Toads of Grimmerdale! One of the many stories about the remnants of those other people, or things, which had already mostly faded from this land, so that the coming of man did not dislodge them, for the land had been largely deserted before the first settlement ship arrived.

Still there were places in plenty where certain powers and presences were felt to this day, where things could be invoked—by men who were crazed enough to summon them. Had the lords of High Hallack not been driven at the last to make such a bargain with the unknown when they signed solemn treaty with the Were Riders? All men knew that it had been the aid of those strange outlanders which had broken the invaders at the last.

Some of the presences were beneficial, others neutral, still others dangerous. Perhaps not actively so in these days. Men were not hunted, harried, or attacked by them. But they had their own places, and the man who was rash enough to trespass there did so at risk.

Among such were the Standing Stones of the Toads of Grimmerdale. The story went that they would answer appeals, but that the manner of answer sometimes did not please the petitioner. For years now men had avoided their place.

But why a shuttered window? If, as according to legend, the toads (people were not sure now if they really *were* toads) did not roam from their portion of the dale, had they once? Making it necessary to bolt and bar against them? And why a second-story window in this dusty room?

Moved by a curiosity he did not wholly understand, Trystan drew his belt knife, pried at the fastenings. They were deeply bitten with rust, and he was sure that the window had not been opened night or day for years. At last the fastenings yielded to his efforts; he was now stubborn about it, somehow even a little angry.

Even though he was at last able to withdraw the bar, he had a second struggle with the warped wood, finally using sword point to lever it. The shutters grated open, the chill of the night entered, making him aware at once of how very odorous and sour was the fog within.

Trystan looked out upon snow and a straggle of dark trees, with the upslope of the dale wall beyond. There were no other buildings set between the inn and that rise. And the thick vegetation showing dark above the sweep of white on the ground suggested that the land was uncultivated. The trees there were not tall, it was mainly brush, alone and he did not like it.

His war-trained instincts saw there a menace. Any enemy could creep in its cover to within a spear-cast of the inn. Yet perhaps those of Grimmerdale did not have such fears, and so saw no reason to grub out and burn there.

The slope began gradually and shortly the tangled growth thinned out, as if someone had there taken the precautions Trystan thought right. Above was smooth snow, very white and unbroken in the moonlight. Then came outcrops of rock. But after he had studied those with an eye taught to take quick inventory of a countryside, he was sure they were no natural formations but had been set with a purpose.

They did not form a connected wall. There were wide spaces between as if they had served as posts for some stringing of fence. Yet for that they were extra thick.

And the first row led to a series of five such lines, though in successive rows the stones were placed closer and closer together. Trystan was aware of two things. One, bright as the moon was, it did not, he was sure, account for all the light among the stones. There was a radiance which seemed to rise either from them or the ground about them. Second, no snow lay on the land from the point where the lines of rock pillar began. And above the stones there was a misting, as if something there bewildered or hindered clear sight.

Trystan blinked, rubbed his hand across his eyes, looked again. The clouding was more pronounced when he did so. As if whatever lay there increased the longer he watched it.

That this was not of human Grimmerdale he was certain. It had all the signs of being one of those strange places where old powers lingered. And that this was the refuge or stronghold of the "toads" he was now sure. That the shutter had been bolted against the weird sight he could also understand, and he rammed and pounded the warped wood back into place, though he could not reset the bar he had levered out.

Slowly he put aside mail and outer clothing, laying it across the chest. He spread out the bedding over the hide webbing. Surprisingly the rough sheets, the two woven covers were clean. They even (now that he had drawn lungfuls of fresh air to awaken his sense of smell) were fragrant with some kind of herb.

Trystan stretched out, pulled the covers about his ears, drowsy and content, willing himself to sleep.

He awoke to a clatter at the door. At first he frowned up at the cobwebbed rafters above. What had he dreamed? Deep in his mind there was a troubled feeling, a sense that a message of some importance had been lost. He shook his head against such fancies and padded to the door, opened it for the entrance of the elder serving man, a dour-faced, skeleton-thin fellow who was more cleanly of person than the pot boy. He carried a covered kettle which he put down on the chest before he spoke.

"Water for washing, master. There be grain mush, pig cheek, and ale below."

"Well enough." Trystan slid the lid off the pot. Steam curled up. He had not expected this small luxury, and he took its arrival as an omen of fortune for the day.

Below the long room was empty. The lame boy was washing off table tops, splashing water on the floor in great scummy dollops.

His mistress stood, hands on her hips, her elbows outspread like crooked wings, her sharp chin with its two haired warts outthrust like a spear to threaten the woman before her, well cloaked against the outside winter, but with her hood thrown back to expose her face.

That face was thin, with sharp features lacking any claim to comeliness, since the stretched skin was mottled with unsightly brown patches. But her cloak, Trystan saw, was good wool, certainly not that of a peasant wench. She carried a bundle in one hand, and in the other was a short-hafted hunting spear, its butt scarred as if it had served her more as a journey staff than a weapon.

"Well enough, wench. But here you work for the food in your mouth, the clothing on your back." The mistress shot a single glance at Trystan before she centered her attention once more on the girl.

Girl, Trystan thought she was. Though by the Favor of Likerwolf certainly her face was not that of a dewy maid, being rather enough to turn a man's thoughts more quickly to other things when he looked upon her.

"Put your gear on the shelf yonder," the mistress gestured. "Then come to work, if you speak the truth on wanting that."

She did not watch to see her orders obeyed, but came to the table where Trystan had seated himself.

"Grain mush, master. And a slicing of pig jowl—ale fresh drawn—"

He nodded, sitting much as he had the night before, fingering the finely wrought guard about his wrist, his eyes half closed as if he were still wearied, or else turned his thoughts on things not about him.

The mistress stumped away. But he was not aware she had returned until someone slid a tray onto the table. It was the girl, her shrouding of cloak gone, so that the tight bodice of the pleated skirt could be seen. And he was right; she did not wear peasant clothes, that was a skirt divided for riding, though it had now been shortened enough to show boots, scuffed and worn, straw protruding from their tops. Her figure was thin, yet shapely enough to make a man wonder at the fate which wedded such to that horror of a face. She did not need her spear for protection; all she need do was show her face to any would-be ravisher and she would be as safe as the statue of Gunnora the farmers carried through their fields at first sowing.

"Your food, master." She was deft, far more so than the mistress, as she slid the platter of crisp browned mush and thin-sliced pink meat onto the board.

"Thanks given," Trystan found himself making civil answer as he might in some keep were one of the damosels there noticing him in courtesy.

He reached for the tankard and at that moment saw her head sway, her eyes wide open rested on his hand. And he thought, with a start of surprise, that her interest was no slight one. But when he looked again she was moving away, her eyes downcast like those of any proper serving wench.

"There will be more, master?" she asked in a colorless voice. But her voice also betrayed her. No girl save one hold bred would have such an accent.

There had been many upsets in the dales. What was it to him if some keep woman had been flung out of her soft nest to tramp the roads, serve in an inn for bread and a roof? With her face she could not hope to catch a man to fend for her—unless he be struck blind before their meeting.

"No," he told her. She walked away with the light and soundless step of a forest hunter, the grace of one who sat at high tables by right of blood.

Well, he, too, would sit at a high table come next year's end. Of that he was as certain as if it had been laid upon him by some Power Master as an unbreakable geas. But it would be because of his own two hands, the cunning of his mind, and as such his rise would be worth more than blood right. She had come down, he would go up. Seeing her made him just more confident of the need for moving on with his plan.

3

THE ROAD along the ridges was even harder footing after Norden-dale, Hertha discovered. There were gaps where landslides had cut away sections, making the going very slow. However she kept on, certain this was the only way to approach what she sought.

As she climbed and slid, edged with caution, even in places had to leap recklessly with her spear as a vaulting pole, she considered what might lie ahead. In seeking Gunnora she had kept to the beliefs of her people. But if she continued to the shrine of the Toads she turned her back on what safety she knew.

Around her neck was hung a small bag of grain and dried herbs, Gunnora's talisman for home and hearth. Another such was sewn into the breast of her undersmock. And in the straw which lined each boot were other leaves with their protection for the wayfarer. Before she had set out on this journey she had marshaled all she knew of protective charms.

But whether such held against alien powers, she could not tell. To each race its own magic. The old ones were not men, and their beliefs and customs must have been far different. That being so, did she now tempt great evil?

Always when she reached that point she remembered. And memory was as sharp as any spur on a rider's heel. She had been going to the abbey in Lethendale, Kuno having suggested it. Perhaps that was why he had turned from her, feeling guilt in the matter.

Going to Lethendale, she must ever remember how it was, every dark part of it. For if she did not hold that in mind, then she would lose the bolster of anger for her courage. A small party because Kuno was sure there was naught to fear from the fleeing invaders. But after all it was not the invaders she had to fear.

There had come a rain of arrows out of nowhere. She could hear yet the bubbling cry of young Jannesk as he fell from the saddle with one through his throat. They had not even seen the attackers, and all the men had been shot down in only moments. She had urged her mount on, only to have him entangle hoofs in a trip rope. After that she could remember only flying over his head—

Until she awoke in the dark, her hands tied, looking out into a clearing where a fire burned between rocks. Men sat about the fire tearing at chunks of half-roasted meat. *Those* had been the invaders. And she had lain cold, knowing well what they meant for her when they had satisfied one appetite and were ready—

They had come to her at last. Even with tied hands she had fought. So they had laughed and cuffed her among them, tearing at her garments and handling her shamefully, though they did not have time for the last insult and degradation of all. No, that was left for some—some *man* of her own people!

Thinking on it now made rage rise to warm her even though the sun had withdrawn from this slope and there was a chill rising wind.

For the ambushers had been attacked in turn, fell under spear and arrow out of the dark. Half conscious she had been left lying until a harsh weight on her, hard, bruising hands brought her back to terror and pain.

She had never seen his face, but she had seen (and it was branded on her memory for all time) the bow guard encircling the wrist tightened as a bar across her throat to choke her unconscious. And when she had once more stirred she was alone.

Someone had thrown a cloak over her nakedness. There was a horse nearby. There was for the rest only dead men under a falling snow. She never understood why they had not killed her and been done with it. Perhaps in that little her attacker had been overridden by his companions. But at the time she had been sorely tempted

122

to lie where she was and let the cold put an end to her. Only the return of that temper which was her heritage roused her. Somewhere living was the man who should have been her savior and instead had rift from her what was to be given only as a free gift. To bring him down, for that she would live.

Later, when she found she carried new life, yes, she had been tempted again—to do as they urged, rid herself of that. But in the end she could not. For though part of the child was of evil, yet a part was hers. Then she recalled Gunnora and the magic which could aid. So she had withstood Kuno's urging, even his brutal anger.

She held to two things with all the stubborn strength she could muster—that she would bear this child which must be hers only, and that she would have justice on the man who would never in truth be its father. The first part of her desire Gunnora had given. Now she went for answer to the second.

At last night came and she found a place among the rocks where she could creep in, the stone walls giving refuge from the wind, a carpet of dried leaves to blanket her. She must have slept, for when she roused she was not sure where she was. Then she was aware of the influence which must have brought her awake. There was an uneasiness of the very air about her, a tension as if she stood on the verge of some great event.

With the spear as her staff, Hertha came farther into the open. The moon showed her unmarked snow ahead, made dark pits of her own tracks leading here. With it for a light she started on.

A wan radiance, having no light of fire, shown in the distance. It came from no torch either, she was sure. But it might well mark what she sought.

Here the Old Road was unbroken though narrow. She prodded the snow ahead, lest there be some hidden crevice. But she hurried as if to some important meeting.

Tall shapes arose, stones set on end in rows. In the outer lines there were wide spaces between, but the stones of the inner rows

123

were placed closer and closer together. She followed a road cut straight between these pillars.

On the crest of each rested a small cone of light, as if these were not rocks but giant candles to light her way. And that light was cold instead of warm, blue instead of the orange-red of true flame. Also here the moonlight was gone, so that even though there was no roof she could see, yet it was shut away.

Three stone rows she passed, then four more, each with the stones closer together, so that the seventh brought them touching to form a wall. The road dwindled to a path which led through a gate in the wall.

Hertha knew that even had she wanted to retreat, now she could not. It was as if her feet were held to the path and it moved, bearing her with it.

So she came into a hexagonal space within the wall. There was a low curbing of stone to fence off the centermost portion and in each angle blazed a flame at ground level. But she could go no farther, just as she could not draw away.

Within the walled area were five blocks of green stone. These glistened in the weird light as if they were carved of polished gems. Their tops had been squared off to give seating for those who awaited her.

What she had expected Hertha was not sure. But what she saw was so alien to all she knew that she did not even feel fear, but rather wonder that such could exist in a world where men also walked. Now she could understand why these bore the name of toads, for that was the closest mankind could come in descriptive comparison.

Whether they went on two limbs or four she could not be sure the way they hunched upon their blocks. But they were no toads in spite of their resemblance. Their bodies were bloated of paunch, the four limbs seemingly too slender beside that heaviness. Their heads sat upon narrow shoulders with no division of neck. And those heads were massive, with large golden eyes high on their hairless skulls, noses which were slits only, and wide mouths stretching above only a vestige of chin.

"Welcome, seeker—"

The words rang in her head, not her ears. Nor could she tell which of the creatures had addressed her.

Now that Hertha had reached her goal she found no words, she was too bemused by the sight of those she had sought. Yet it seemed that she did not have to explain, for the mind speech continued:

"You have come seeking our aid. What would you, daughter of men—lose that which weighs your body?"

At that Hertha found her tongue to speak.

"Not so. Though the seed in me was planted not by lawful custom but in pain and torment of mind and body, yet will I retain it. I shall bear a child who shall be mine alone, as Gunnora has answered my prayers."

"Then what seek you here?"

"Justice! Justice upon him who took me by force and in shame!"

"Why think you, daughter of men, that you and your matters mean aught to us, who were great in this land before your feeble kind came and who will continue to abide even after man is again gone? What have we to do with you?"

"I do not know. Only I have listened to old tales, and I have come."

She had an odd sensation then, if one could sense laughter in one's mind, she was feeling it. They were amused, and knowing that she lost some of her assurance.

Again a surge of amusement, and then a feeling as if they had withdrawn, conferred among themselves. Hertha would have fled, but she could not. And she was afraid as she had not been since she faced horror on the road to Lethendale.

"Upon whom ask you justice, daughter of men? What is his name, where lies he this night?"

She answered with the truth. "I know neither. I have not even seen his face. Yet"—she forgot her fear, knew only that which goaded her on, "I have that which shall make him known to me. And I may find him here in Grimmerdale, since men in many now pass along this road, the war being ended."

Again that withdrawal. Then another question.

"Do you not know that services such as ours do not come without payment? What have you to offer us in return, daughter of men?"

Hertha was startled, she had never really thought past making her plea here. That she had been so stupid amazed her. Of course there would be payment! Instinctively she dropped her bundle, clasped her hands in guard over where the child lay.

Amusement once more.

"Nay, daughter of men. From Gunnora you have claimed that life, nor do we want it. But justice can serve us too. We shall give you the key to that which you wish, and the end shall be ours. To this do you agree?"

"I do." Though she did not quite understand.

"Look you—there!" One of the beings raised a forefoot and pointed over her shoulder. Hertha turned her head. There was a small glowing spot on the surface of the stone pillar. She put out her hand and at her touch a bit of stone loosened, so she held a small pebble.

"Take that, daughter of men. When you find him you seek, see it lies in his bed at the coming of night. Then your justice will fall upon him—here! And you will not forget, nor think again and change your mind, we shall set a reminder where you shall see it each time you look into your mirror."

Again the being pointed, this time at Hertha. From the forelimb curled a thin line of vapor. That gathered to form a ball which flew at her. Though she flinched and tried to duck, it broke against her face with a tingling feeling which lasted only for a second.

"You shall wear that until he comes hither, daughter of men. So will you remember your bargain."

What happened then she was not sure, it was all confused. When she was clearheaded again dawn was breaking, and she clawed her way out of the leaf-carpeted crevice. Was it all a dream? No, her fingers were tight about something, cramped and in pain from that hold. She looked down at a pebble of green-gray stone. So in truth she had met the Toads of Grimmerdale.

Grimmerdale itself lay spread before her, easy to see in the gathering light. The lord's castle was on the farther slope, the village and inn by the highway. And it was the inn she must reach.

Early as it was there were signs of life about the place. A man went to the stable without noticing her as she entered the courtyard. She advanced to the half-open door, determined to strike some bargain for work with the mistress, no matter how difficult the woman was reputed to be.

The great room was empty when she entered. But moments later a woman with a forbidding face stumped in. Hertha went directly to her. The woman stared at her and then grinned maliciously.

"You've no face to make trouble, wench, one can be certain of that," she said when Hertha asked for work. "And it is true that an extra pair of hands is wanted. Not that we have a purse so fat we can toss away silver—"

As she spoke a man came down the steep inner stair, crossed to sit at a table half screened from the rest. It was almost as if his arrival turned the scales in Hertha's favor. For she was told to put aside her bundle and get to work. So it was she who took the food tray to where he sat.

He was tall, taller than Kuno, with well-set, wide shoulders. And there was a sword by his side, plain-hilted, in a worn scabbard. His features were sharp, his face thin, as if he might have gone on short rations too often in the past. Black hair peaked on his forehead and she could not guess his age, though she thought he might be young.

But it was when she put down her tray and he reached out for an eating knife that it seemed the world stopped for an instant. She saw the bowguard on his wrist. And her whole existence narrowed to that metal band. Some primitive instinct of safety closed about her, she was sure she had not betrayed herself.

As she turned from the table she wondered if this was by the power of the Toads, if they had brought her prey to her hand so. What had they bade her—to see that the pebble was in his bed. But this was early morn and he had just risen, what if he meant not to stay another night but would push on? How could she then carry out their orders? Unless she followed after him, somehow crept upon him at nightfall.

At any rate he seemed in no hurry to be up and off, if that was his purpose. Finally, with relief, she heard him bargain with the mistress for a second night's stay. She found an excuse to go above, carrying fresh bedding for a second room to be made ready. And as she went down the narrow hall she wondered how best she could discover which room was his.

So intent was she upon this problem that she was not aware of someone behind her until an ungentle hand fell on her shoulder and she was jerked about.

"Now here's a new one—" The voice was brash and young. Hertha looked at a man with something of the unformed boy still in his face. His thick yellow hair was uncombed, his jaw beard stubbled, his eyes red-rimmed.

As he saw her clearly he made a grimace of distaste, shoved her from him with force, so she lost her balance and fell to the floor.

"—leave kiss a toad!" He spat, but the trail of spittle never struck her. Instead hands fell on him, slammed him against the other wall. While the man of the bowguard surveyed him steadily.

"What's to do?" The younger man struggled. "Take your hands off me, fellow!"

"Fellow, is it?" observed the other. "I am no liegeman of yours, Urre. Nor are you in Roxdale now. As for the wench, she's not to blame for her face. Perhaps she should thank whatever Powers she lights a candle to that she had it. With such as you ready to lift every skirt they meet."

128

"Toad! She is a toad-face—" Urre worked his mouth as if he wished to spit again, then something in the other's eyes must have warned him. "Hands off me!" He twisted and the other stepped back. With an oath Urre lurched away, heading unsteadily for the stair.

Hertha got to her feet, stooped to gather up the draggle of covers she had dropped.

"Has he hurt you?"

She shook her head dumbly. It had all been so sudden, and that *he*—this one—had lifted hand in her defense dazed her. She moved away as fast as she could, but before she reached the end of the passage she looked back. He was going through a door a pace away from where the one called Urre had stopped her. So—she had learned his room. But "toad-face"? That wet ball which had struck her last night—what had it done to her?

Hertha used her fingers to trace any alteration in her features. But to her touch she was as she had always been. A mirror—she must find a mirror! Not that the inn was likely to house such a luxury.

In the end she found one in the kitchen, in a tray which she had been set to polishing. Though her reflection was cloudy, there was no mistaking the ugly brown patches on her skin. Would they be so forever, a brand set by her trafficking with dark powers, or would they vanish with the task done? Something she had remembered from that strange voiceless conversation made her hope the latter was true.

If so, the quicker she moved to the end the better. But she did not soon get another chance to slip aloft. The man's name was Trystan. The lame pot boy had taken an interest in him and was full of information. Trystan had been a Marshal and a Master of Archers—he was now out of employment, moving inland probably to seek a new lord. But perhaps he was thinking of raising a war band on his own; he had talked already with other veterans staying here. He did not drink much, though those others with him,

Urre, who was son to a dale lord, and his liegeman ordered enough to sink a ship.

Crumbs, yes, but she listened eagerly for them, determined to learn all she could of this Trystan she must enmesh in her web. She watched him, too, given occasion when she might do so without note. It gave her a queer feeling to look this way upon the man who had used her so and did not guess now she was so near.

Oddly enough, had it not been for the evidence of the bowguard she would have picked him last of those she saw beneath this roof. Urre, yes, and two or three others, willing to make free with her until they saw her face clearly. But when she had reason to pass by this Trystan he showed her small courtesies, as if her lack of comeliness meant nothing. He presented a puzzle which was disturbing.

But that did not change her plan. So, at last, when she managed close to dusk to slip up the stairway quickly, she sped down the hall to his room. There was a huddle of coverings on the bed. She could not straighten them, but she thrust the pebble deep into the bag-pillow and hurried back to the common room, where men were gathering. There she obeyed a stream of orders, fetching and carrying tankards of drink, platters of food.

The fatigue of her long day of unaccustomed labor was beginning to tell. And there were those among the patrons who used cruel humor to enliven the evening. She had to be keenwitted and cleareyed to avoid a foot slyly thrust forth to trip her, a sudden grab at her arm to dump a filled platter or tray of tankards. Twice she suffered defeat and was paid by a ringing buffet from the mistress' hand for the wasting of food.

But at length she was freed from their persecution by the mistress (not out of any feeling for her, but as a matter of saving spillage and spoilage) and set to the cleaning of plates in a noisome hole where the stench of old food and greasy slops turned her stomach and made her so ill she was afraid she could not last. Somehow she held out until finally the mistress sourly shoved her to one of the fireside settles and told her that was the best bed she could hope for. Hertha curled up, so tired she ached, while the rest of the inn people dragged off to their holes and corners—chambers were for guests alone.

The fire had been banked for the night, but the hearth was warm. Now that she had the great room to herself, though her body was tired, her mind was alert, and she rested as best she could while she waited. If all went well, surely the stone would act this night, and she determined to witness the action. Beyond that she had not planned.

Hertha waited for what seemed a long time, shifting now and then on her hard bed. Near to hand were both her cloak and the spear staff, her boots, new filled with fresh straw, were on her feet.

She was aware of a shadow at the head of the stairs, or steps. She watched and listened. Yes, she had been right—this was the man Trystan, and he was walking toward the door. Whirling her cloak about her, Hertha rose to follow.

4

SHE CLUNG to the shadow of the inn wall for fear he might look behind. But he strode on with the sure step of a man on some mission of such importance his present surroundings had little meaning, rounding the back of the inn, tramping upslope.

Though a moon hung overhead, there was also a veiling of cloud. Hertha dropped farther and farther behind, for the brambles of the scrub caught at her cloak, the snow weighted her skirt, and the fatigue of her long day's labor was heavy on her. Yet she felt that she must be near to Trystan when he reached his goal. Was it that she must witness the justice of the Toads? She was not sure any more, concentrating all her effort on the going.

Now she could see the stones stark above. They bore no candles on their crests this night, were only grim blots of darkness. Toward them Trystan headed in as straight a line as the growth would allow.

He reached the first line of stones; not once had he looked around. Long since Hertha abandoned caution. He was almost out of sight! She gathered up her skirts, panting heavily as she plunged and skidded to where he had disappeared.

Yes, now she could see him, though he was well ahead. But when he reached that final row, the one forming a real wall, he would have to move along it to the entrance of the Old Road. While she, already knowing the way, might gain a few precious moments by seeking the road now. And she did that, coming to better footing with her breath whistling through her lips in gasps.

She had no spear to lean on and she nursed a sharp pain in her side. But she set her teeth and wavered on between those rows of stones, seeing the gate ahead and in it a dark figure. Trystan was still a little before.

There came a glow of light, the cold flames were back on pillar top. In its blue radiance her hands looked diseased and foul when she put them out to steady herself as she went.

Trystan was just within the gate of the hexagon. He had not moved, but rather stared straight ahead at whatever awaited him. His sword was belted at his side, the curve of his bow was a pointing finger behind his shoulder. He had come fully armed, yet he made no move to draw weapon now.

Hertha stumbled on. That struggle upslope had taken much of her strength. Yet in her was the knowledge that she must be there. Before her now, just beyond her touching even if she reached forth her arm, was Trystan. His head was uncovered, the loose hood of his surcoat lay back on his shoulders. His arms dangled loosely at his sides. Hertha's gaze followed to the object of his staring concentration.

There were the green blocks. But no toad forms humped upon them. Rather lights played there, weaving in and out in a flickering dance of shades of blue—from a wan blight which might have emanated from some decaying bit on a forest floor, to a brilliant sapphire.

Hertha felt the pull of those weaving patterns until she forced herself (literally forced her heavy hands to cover her eyes) not to look upon the play of color. When she did so there was a sensation of release. But it was plain her companion was fast caught.

Cupping her hands to shut out all she could of the lights, she watched Trystan. He made no move to step across the low curbing and approach the blocks. He might have been turned into stone himself, rapt in a spell which had made of him ageless rock. He did not blink an eye, nor could she even detect the rise and fall of his chest in breathing.

Was this their judgment then, the making of a man into a motionless statue? Somehow Hertha was sure that whatever use the Toads intended to make of the man they had entrapped through her aid, it was more than this. Down inside her something stirred. Angrily she fought against that awakening of an unbidden thought, or was it merely emotion? She drew memory to her, lashed herself with all shameful, degrading detail. This had he done to her and this and this! By his act she was homeless, landless, a nothing, wearing even a toad face. Whatever came now to him, he richly deserved it. She would wait and watch, and then she would go hence, and in time, as Gunnora had promised, she would bear a son or daughter who had none of this father—none!

Still watching him, her hands veiling against the play of the ensorcelling light, Hertha saw his lax fingers move, clench into a fist. And then she witnessed the great effort of that gesture, and she knew that he was in battle, silent though he stood, that he fought with all his strength against what held him fast.

That part of her which had stirred and awakened grew stronger. She battled it. He deserved nothing but what would come to him here, he deserved nothing from her but the justice she had asked from the Toads.

His fist arose, so slowly that it might have been chained to some great weight. When Hertha looked from it to his face she saw the agony the movement was causing him. She set her shoulders to the rock wall—had she but a rope she would have bound herself there, that no weakness might betray her plan.

Strange light before him and something else, formless as yet, but with a cold menace greater than any fear born of battle heat. For this terror was rooted not in any ordinary danger, but grew from a horror belonging by rights far back in the beginnings of his race. How he had come here, whether this be a dream or no, Trystan was not sure. And he had no time to waste on confused memory.

What energy he possessed must be used to front that which was keeping him captive. It strove to fill him with its own life, and that he would not allow, not while he could summon will to withstand it.

Somehow he thought that if he broke the hold upon his body, he could also shatter its would-be mastery of his mind and will. Could he act against its desires, he might regain control. So he set full concentration on his hand—his fingers. It was as if his flesh were nerveless, numb— But he formed a fist. Then he brought up his arm, so slowly that had he allowed himself to waver he might have despaired. But he knew that he must not relax the intense drive of will centered in that simple move. Weapons—what good would his bow, his sword be against what dwelt here? He sensed dimly that this menace could well laugh at weapons forged and carried by those of his kind.

Weapons—sword—steel—there was something hovering just at the fringe of memory. Then for an instant he saw a small, sharp mind picture. Steel! That man from the Waste-side dale who had set his sword as a barrier at the head of his sleeping roll, plunged his dagger point deep in the soil at his feet the night they had left him on the edge of very ancient ruins with their mounts. Between cold iron a man lay safe, he said. Some scoffed at his superstition, others had nodded agreement. Iron—cold iron—which certain old Powers feared.

He had a sword at his belt now, a long dagger at his hip—iron —talisman? But the struggle of possession of his fist, his arm was so hard he feared he would never have a chance to put the old belief to the proof.

What did they want of him, those who abode here? For he was aware that there was more than one will bent on him. Why had they brought him? Trystan shied away from questions. He must concentrate on his hand—his arm!

With agonizing slowness he brought his hand to his belt, forced his fingers to touch the hilt of his sword.

That was no lord's proud weapon with a silvered, jeweled hilt, but a serviceable blade nicked and scratched by long use. So that the hilt itself was metal, wound with thick wire to make a good grip which would not turn in a sweating hand. His finger tips touched that and—his hand was free!

He tightened hold instantly, drew the blade with a practiced sweep, and held it up between him and that riot of blending and weaving blue lights. Relief came, but it was only minor he knew after a moment or two of swelling hope. What coiled here could not be so easily defeated. Always that other will weighted and plucked at his hand. The sword blade swung back and forth, he was unable to hold it steady. Soon he might not be able to continue to hold it at all!

Trystan tried to retreat even a single step. But his feet were as if set in a bog, entrapped against any move. He had only his failing hand and the sword, growing heavier every second. Now he was not holding it erect as if on guard, but doubled back as if aimed at his own body!

Out of the blue lights arose a tendril of wan phosphorescent stuff

135

which looped into the air and held there, its tip pointed in his direction. Another weaved up to join it, swell its substance. A third came, a fourth was growing—

The tip, which had been narrow as a finger, was now thickening. From that smaller tips rounded and swelled into being. Suddenly Trystan was looking at a thing of active evil, a grotesque copy of a human hand, four fingers, a thumb too long and thin.

When it was fully formed it began to lower toward him. Trystan with all his strength brought up the sword, held its point as steady as he could against that reaching hand.

Again he knew a fleeting triumph. For at the threat of the sword, the hand's advance was stayed. Then it moved right, left, as if to strike as a foeman's point past his guard. But he was able by some miracle of last reserves to counter each attack.

Hertha watched the strange duel wide-eyed. The face of her enemy was wet, great trickles of sweat ran from his forehead to drip from his chin. His mouth was a tight snarl, lips flattened against his teeth. Yet he held that sword and the emanation of the Toads could not pass it.

"You!"

The word rang in her head with a cold arrogance which hurt.

"Take from him the sword!"

An order she must obey if she was to witness her triumph. Her triumph? Hertha crouched against the rock watching that weird battle—sword point swinging with such painful slowness, but ever just reaching the right point in time so that the blue hand did not close. The man was moving so slowly, why could the Toads not beat him by a swift dart past his guard? Unless their formation of the hand, their use of it was as great an effort for them as his defense seemed to be for him.

"The sword!" That demand in her mind hurt.

Hertha did not stir. "I cannot!" Did she cry that aloud, whisper it, or only think it? She was not sure. Nor why she could not carry through to the end that which had brought her here—that she did not understand either.

Dark—and her hands were bound. There were men struggling. One went down with an arrow through him. Then cries of triumph. Someone came to her through shadows. She could see only mail—a sword—

Then she was pinned down by a heavy hand. She heard laughter, evil laughter which scorched her, though her body shivered as the last of her clothing was ripped away. Once more—

NO! She would not remember it all! She would not! They could not make her—but they did. Then she was back in the here and now. And she saw Trystan fighting his stumbling, hopeless battle, knew him again for what he was.

"The sword—take from him the sword!"

Hertha lurched to her feet. The sword—she must get the sword. Then he, too, would learn what it meant to be helpless and shamed and—and what? Dead? Did the Toads intend to kill him?

"Will you kill him?" she asked them. She had never foreseen the reckoning to be like this.

"The sword!"

They did not answer, merely spurred her to their will. Death? No, she was certain they did not mean his death, at least not death such as her kind knew it. And—but—

"The sword!"

In her mind that order was a painful lash, meant to send her unthinking to their service. But it acted otherwise, alerting her to a new sense of peril. She had evoked that which had no common meeting with her kind. Now she realized she had loosed that which not even the most powerful man or woman she knew might meddle with. Trystan could deserve the worst she was able to pull upon him. But that must be the worst by men's standards—not this!

Her left hand went to the bag of Gunnora's herbs where it rested between her swelling breasts. Her right groped on the ground, closed about a stone. Since she touched the herb bag that voice was no longer a pain in her head. It faded like a far-off calling. She readied the stone—

Trystan watched that swinging hand. His sword arm ached up into his shoulder. He was sure every moment he would lose control. Hertha bent, tore at the lacing of her bodice so that the herb bag swung free. Fiercely she rubbed it back and forth on the stone. What so pitiful an effort might do—

She threw it through the murky air, struck against that blue hand. It changed direction, made a dart past him. Knowing that this might be his one chance, Trystan brought down the sword with all the force he could muster on the tentacle which supported the hand.

The blade passed through as if what he saw had no substance, had been woven of his own fears. There was a burst of pallid light. Then the lumpish hand, and that which supported it, were gone.

In the same moment he discovered he could move, and staggered back. And a hand fell upon his arm, jerking him in the same direction. He flailed out wildly at what could only be an enemy's hold, broke it. There was a cry and he turned his head.

A dark huddle lay at the foot of the stone door frame. Trystan advanced the sword point, ready, as strength flowed once more into him, to meet this new attack. The bundle moved, a white hand clutched at the pillar, pulled.

His bemused mind cleared. This was a woman! Not only that, but what had passed him through the air had not been flung at him, but at the hand. She had been a friend and not an enemy in that moment.

But now from behind he heard a new sound, like the hiss of a disturbed serpent. Or there might be more than one snake voicing hate. He gained the side of the woman, with the rock at his back, looked once more at the center space.

That tentacle which had vanished at the sword-stroke might be gone, but there were others rising. And this time the tentacles did not unite to form hands, but rather each produced something like

138

unto a serpent head. And they arose in such numbers that no one man could stand to front them all— Though he must try.

Once more he felt a light weight upon his shoulder, he glanced to the side. The woman was standing, one hand tight to her breast, the other resting on his upper arm now. Her hood overshadowed her face so he could not see it. But he could hear the murmur of her voice even through the hissing of the pseudo-serpents. Though he could not understand the words, there was a rhythmic flow as if she chanted a battle song for his encouragement.

One of the serpent lengths swung at them, he used the sword. At its touch the thing vanished. But one out of a dozen, what was that? Again his arm grew heavy, he found movement difficult.

Trystan tried to shake off the woman's hold, not daring to take a hand from his sword to repell her.

"Loose me!" he demanded, twisting his body.

She did not obey, nor answer. He heard only that murmur of sound. There was a pleading note in it, a frantic pleading, he could feel her urgency, as if she begged of someone aid for them both.

Then from where her fingers dug into his shoulder muscles there spread downward along his arm, across his back and chest a warmth, a loosing—not of her hold, but of the bonds laid on him here. And within the center space the snake heads darted with greater vigor. Now and then two met in midair, and when they did they instantly united, becoming larger.

These darted forth, striking at the two by the gate, while Trystan cut and parried. And they moved with greater speed so he was hard put to keep them off. They showed no poison fangs, nor did they even seem to have teeth within their open jaws. Yet he sensed that if those mouths closed upon him or the woman they would be utterly done.

He half turned to beat off one which had come at him from an angle. His foot slipped and he went to one knee, the sword half out of his grasp. As he grabbed it tighter he heard a cry. Still crouched he slewed around.

The serpent head at which he had struck had only been a ruse. For his lunge at it had carried him away from the woman. Two other heads had captured her. To his horror he saw that one had fastened across her head, engulfing most of it on contact. The other had snapped its length of body about her waist. Gagged by the one on her head she was quiet, nor did she struggle as the pallid lengths pulled her back to the snakes' lair. Two more reached out to fasten upon her, no longer heeding Trystan, intent on their capture.

He cried out hoarsely, was on his feet again striking savagely at those dragging her. Then he was startled by a voice which seemed to speak within his head.

"Draw back, son of men, lest we remember our broken bargain. This is no longer your affair."

"Loose her!" Trystan cut at the tentacle about her waist. It burst into light, but another was already taking its place.

"She delivered you to us, would you save her?"

"Loose her!" He did not stop to weigh the right or wrong of what had been said, he only knew that he would not see the woman drawn to that which waited—that he could not do and remain a man. He thrust again.

The serpent coils were moving faster, drawing back into the hexagon. Trystan could not even be sure she still lived, not with that dreadful thing upon her head. She hung limp, not fighting.

"She is ours! Go you—lest we take more for feasting."

Trystan wasted no breath in argument, he leaped to the left, mounting the curb of the hexagon. There he slashed into the coils which pulled at the woman. His arms were weak, he could hardly raise the sword, even two-handed, and bring it down. Yet still he fought stubbornly to cut her free. And little by little he thought that he was winning.

Now he noted that as the coils tightened about her they did not touch her hand where it still rested clasping something between her breasts. So he strove the more to cut the coils below, severing the last as her head and shoulders were pulled over the edge of the curb.

Then it seemed that, tug though they would, the tentacles could not drag her wholly in. As they fought to do so Trystan had his last small grant of time. He now hewed those which imprisoned her head and shoulders. Others were rising for new holds. But, as she so lay, to do their will they must reach across her breast to take hold, and that they apparently could not do.

Wearily he raised the blade and brought it down again, each time sure he could not do so again. But at last there was a moment when she was free of them all. He flung out his left hand, clasped hers where it lay between her breasts, heaved her back and away.

There was a sharp hissing from the serpent things. They writhed and twisted. But more and more they sank to the ground, rolled there feebly. He got the woman on his shoulder, tottered back, still facing the enemy, readied as best he could be for another attack.

5

IT WOULD seem that the enemy was spent, at least the snakes did not strike outward again. Watching them warily, Trystan retreated, dared to stop and rest with the woman. He leaned above her to touch her cheek. To his fingers the flesh was cold, faintly clammy. Dead? Had the air been choked from her?

He burrowed beneath the edges of her hood, sought the pulse in her throat. He could find none, so he tried to lay his hand directly above her heart. In doing so he had to break her grip on what lay between her breasts. When he touched a small bag there a throbbing, a warmth spread up his hand, and he jerked hastily away before he realized this was not a danger but a source of energy and life.

Her heart still beat. Best get her well away while those things in the hexagon were quiescent. For he feared their defeat was only momentary.

Trystan dared to sheath his sword, leaving both arms free to carry the woman. For all the bulk of her cloak and clothing she was slender, less than the weight he expected.

Now his retreat was that of a coastal sea crab, keeping part attention on the stew pot of blue light at his back, part on the footing ahead. And he drew a full breath again only when he had put two rings of the standing stones between him and the evil they guarded.

Nor was he unaware that there was still something dragging on him, trying to force him to face about. That he battled with will and his sense of self-preservation, his teeth set, a grimace of effort stiffening mouth and jaw.

One by one he pushed past the standing stones. As he went the way grew darker, the weird light fading. And he was beginning to fear that he could no longer trust his own sight. Twice he found himself off the road, making a detour around a pillar which seemed to sprout before him—and thereby heading back the way he had come.

Thus he fought both the compulsion to return and the tricks of vision, learning to fasten his attention on some point only a few steps ahead and wait until he had passed that before he set another goal.

He came at last, the woman resting over his shoulder, into the clean night, the last of the stones behind him. Now he was weak, so weary that he might have made a twenty-four-hour march and fought a brisk skirmish at the end of it. He slipped to his knees, lowered his burden to the surface of the Old Road where, in the open, the wind had scoured the snow away.

There was no moon, the cloud cover was heavy. The woman was now only a dark bulk. Trystan squatted on his heels, his hands dangling loose between his knees, and tried to think coherently.

Of how he had come up here he had no memory at all. He had gone to bed in the normal manner at the inn, first waking to danger when he faced the crawling light in the hexagon. That he had also there fought a danger of the old time he had no doubt at all. But what had drawn him there?

He remembered forcing open the inn window to look upslope. Had that simple curiosity of his been the trigger for this adventure? But that the people of the inn could live unconcerned so close to such a peril—he could hardly believe that. Or because they had lived here so long, were the descendants of men rooted in Grimmerdale, had they developed an immunity to dark forces?

But what had the thing or things in the hexagon said? That she who lay here had delivered him to them. If so—why? Trystan hunched forward on his knees, twitched aside the edge of the hood, stooping very close to look at her. But it was hard to distinguish more than just the general outline of her features in this limited light.

Suddenly her body arched away from him. She screamed with such terror as startled him and pushed against the road under her, her whole attitude one of such agony of fear as held him motionless. Somehow she got to her feet. She had only screamed that once, now he saw her arms move under the hindering folds of her cloak. The moon broke in a thin sliver from under the curtain of the cloud, glinted on what she held in her hand.

Steel swung in an arc for him. Trystan grappled with her before that blade bit into his flesh. She was like a wild thing, twisting, thrusting, kicking, even biting as she fought him. At length he handled her as harshly as he would a man, striking his fist against the side of her chin so her body went limply once more to the road.

There was nothing to do but take her back to the inn. Had her experience in that nest of standing stones affected her brain, turning all about her into enemies? Resigned, he ripped a strip from the hem of her cloak, tied her hands together. Then he got her up so she lay on his back, breathing shallowly, inert. So carrying her he slipped and slid, pushed with difficulty through the scrub to the valley below and the inn.

143

What the hour might be he did not know, but there was a night lantern burning above the door, which swung open at his push. He staggered over to the fireplace, dropped his burden by the hearth, and reached for wood to build up the blaze, wanting nothing now so much as to be warm again.

Hertha's head hurt. The pain seemed to be in the side of her face. She opened her eyes. There was a dim light, but not that wan blue. No, this was flame glow. Someone hunched at the hearth setting wood lengths with expert skill to rebuild the fire. Already there was warmth her body welcomed. She tried to sit up. Only to discover that her wrists were clumsily bound together. Then she tensed, chilled by fear, watching intently him who nursed the fire.

His head was turned from her, she could not see his face, but she had no doubts that it was Trystan. And her last memory—him looming above her, hands outstretched— To take her again as he had that other time! Revulsion sickened her so that she swallowed hurriedly lest she spew openly on the floor. Cautiously she looked around. This was the large room of the inn, he must have carried her back. That he might take his pleasure in a better place than the icy cold of the Old Road? But if he tried that she could scream, fight —surely someone would come—

He looked to her now, watching her so intently that she felt he read easily every one of her confused thoughts.

"I shall kill you," she said distinctly.

"As you tried to do?" He asked that not as if it greatly mattered, but as if he merely wondered.

"Next time I shall not turn aside!"

He laughed. And with that laughter for an instant he seemed another man, one younger, less hardened by time and deeds. "You did not turn aside this time, mistress, I had a hand in the matter." Then that half smile which had come with the laughter faded, and he regarded her with narrowed eyes, his mouth tight set lip to lip.

Hertha refused to allow him to daunt her and glared back. Then he said:

144

"Or are you speaking of something else, mistress? Something which happened before you drew steel on me? Was that—that *thing* right? Did I march to its lair by your doing?"

Somehow she must have given away the truth by some fraction of change he read in her face. He leaned forward and gripped her by the shoulders, dragging her closer to him in spite of her struggles, holding her so they were squarely eye to eye.

"Why? By the Sword Hand of Karther the Fair, why? What did I ever do to you, girl, to make you want to push me into that maw? Or would any man have sufficed to feed those pets? Are they your pets or your masters? Above all, how comes humankind to deal with *them*? And if you so deal, why did you break their spell to aid me? Why, and why, and why!"

He shook her, first gently, and then, with each question, more harshly, so that her head bobbed on her shoulders and she was weak in his hands. Then he seemed to realize that she could not answer him, so he held her tight as if he must read the truth in her eyes as well as hear it from her lips.

"I have no kinsman willing to call you to a sword reckoning," she told him wearily. "Therefore I must deal as best I can. I sought those who might have justice—"

"Justice! Then I was not just a random choice for some purpose of theirs! Yet I swear by the Nine Words of Min, I have never looked upon your face before. Did I in some battle slay close kin— father, brother, lover? But how may that be? Those I fought were the invaders. They had no women save those they rift from the dales. And would any daleswoman extract vengeance for one who was her master-by-force? Or is it that, girl? Did they take you and then you found a lord to your liking among them, forgetting your own blood?"

If she could have she would have spat full in his face for that insult. And he must have read her anger quickly.

"So that is not it. Then why? I am no ruffler who goes about pick-

145

ing quarrels with comrades. Nor have I ever taken any woman who came not to me willingly—"

"No?" She found speech at last, in a hot rush of words. "So you take no woman unwillingly, brave hero? What of three months since on the road to Lethendale? Is it such a usual course of action with you that it can be so lightly put out of mind?"

Angry and fearful though she was, she could see in his expression genuine surprise.

"Lethendale?" he repeated. "Three months since? Girl, I have never been that far north. As to three months ago—I was Marshal of Forces for Lord Ingrim before he fell at the siege of the port."

He spoke so earnestly that she could almost have believed him, had not that bowguard on his wrist proved him false.

"You lie! Yes, you may not know my face. It was in darkness you took me, having overrun the invaders who had taken me captive. My brother's men were all slain. For me they had other plans. But when aid came, then still I was for the taking—as you proved, Marshal!" She made of that a name to be hissed.

"I tell you, I was at the port!" He had released her and she backed against the settle, leaving a good space between them.

"You would swear before a Truth Stone it was me? You know my face, then?"

"I would swear, yes. As for your face—I do not need that. It was in the dark you had your will of me. But there is one proof I carry ever in my mind since that time."

He raised his hand, rubbing fingers along the old scar on his chin, the fire gleamed on the bowguard. That did not match the plainness of his clothing, how could anyone forget seeing it?

"That proof being?"

"You wear it on your wrist, in plain sight. Just as I saw it then, ravisher—your bowguard!"

He held his wrist out, studying the band. "Bowguard! So that is your proof, that made you somehow send me to the Toads." He was half smiling again, but this time cruelly and with no amusement.

"You did send me there, did you not?" He reached forward and before she could dodge pulled the hood fully from her head, stared at her.

"What have you done with the toad-face, girl? Was that some trick of paint, or some magicking you laid on yourself? Much you must have wanted me to so despoil your own seeming to carry through your plan."

She raised her bound hands, touched her cheeks with cold fingers. This time there was no mirror, but if he said the loathsome spotting was gone, then it must be so.

"They did it—" she said, only half comprehending. She had pictured this meeting many times, imagined him saying this or that. He must be very hardened in such matters to hold to this pose of half-amused interest.

"They? You mean the Toads? But now tell me why, having so neatly put me in their power, you were willing to risk your life in my behalf? That I cannot understand. For it seems to me that to traffic with such as abide up that hill is a fearsome thing and one which only the desperate would do. Such desperation is not lightly turned aside—so—why did you save me, girl?"

She answered with the truth. "I do not know. Perhaps because the hurt being mine, the payment should also be mine—that, a little, I think. But even more—" She paused so long he prodded her.

"But even more, girl?"

"I could not in the end leave even such a man as you to *them!*"

"Very well, that I can accept. Hate and fear and despair can drive us all to bargains we repent of later. You made one and then found you were too human to carry it through. Then later on the road you chose to try with honest steel and your own hand—"

"You—you would have taken me—again!" Hertha forced out the words. But the heat in her cheeks came not from the fire but from the old shame eating her.

"So that's what you thought? Perhaps, given the memories you carry, it was natural enough." Trystan nodded. "But now it is your

147

turn to listen to me, girl. Item first: I have never been to Lethendale, three months ago, three years ago—never! Second: this which you have come to judge me on," he held the wrist closer, using the fingers of his other hand to tap upon it, "I did not have three months ago. When the invaders were close pent in the port during the last siege, we had many levies from the outlands come to join us. They had mopped up such raiding bands as had been caught out of there when we moved in to besiege.

"A siege is mainly a time of idleness, and idle men amuse themselves in various ways. We had only to see that the enemy did not break out along the shores while we waited for the coasting ships from Handelsburg and Vennesport to arrive to harry them from the sea. There were many games of chance played during that waiting. And, though I am supposed by most to be a cautious man, little given to such amusements, I was willing to risk a throw now and then.

"This I so won. He who staked it was like Urre, son to some dead lord, with naught but ruins and a lost home to return to if and when the war ended. Two days later he was killed in one of the sorties the invaders now and then made. He had begged me to hold this so that when luck ran again in his way he might buy it back, for it was one of the treasures of his family. In the fighting I discovered it was not only decorative but useful. Since he could not redeem it, being dead, I kept it—to my disfavor it would seem. As for the boy, I do not even know his name—for they called him by some nickname. He was befuddled with drink half the time, being one of the walking dead—"

" 'Walking dead'?" His story carried conviction, not only his words but his tone, and the straight way he told it.

"That is what I call them. High Hallack has them in many—some are youngsters, such as Urre, the owner of this," again he smoothed the guard. "Others are old enough to be their fathers. The dales have been swept with fire and sword. Those which were not invaded have been bled of their men, of their crops—to feed both armies.

This is a land which can now go two ways. It can sink into nothingness from exhaustion, or there can rise new leaders to restore and with will and courage build again."

It seemed to Hertha that he no longer spoke to her, but rather voiced his own thoughts. As for her, there was a kind of emptiness within, as if something she carried had been rift from her. That thought sent her bound hands protectively to her belly.

The child within her—who had been its father? One of the lost ones, some boy who had had all taken from him and so became a dead man with no hope in the future, one without any curb upon his appetites. Doubtless he had lived for the day only, taken ruthlessly all offered during that short day. Thinking so, she again sensed that queer light feeling. She had not lost the child, this child which Gunnora promised would be hers alone. What she had lost was the driving need for justice which had brought her to Grimmerdale—to traffic with the Toads.

Hertha shuddered, cold to her bones in spite of her cloak and the fire. What had she done in her blindness, her hate and horror? Almost she had delivered an innocent man to that she dared not now think upon. What had saved her from that at the very last, made her throw that stone rubbed with Gunnora's talisman? Some part of her that refused to allow such a foul crime?

And what could she ever say to this man who had now turned his head from her, was looking into the flames as if therein he could read message runes? She half raised her bound hands; he looked again with a real smile, from which she shrank as she might from a blow, remembering how it might have been with him at this moment.

"There is no need for you to go bound. Or do you still thirst for my blood?" He caught her hands, pulled at the cloth tying them.

"No," Hertha answered in a low voice. "I believe you. He whom I sought is now dead."

"Do you regret that death came not at your hand?"

She stared down at her fingers resting again against her middle, wondering dully what would become of her now. Would she remain a tavern wench, should she crawl back to Kuno? No! At that her head went up again, pride returned.

"I asked, are you sorry you did not take your knife to my gamester?"

"No."

"But still there are dark thoughts troubling you—"

"Those are none of your concern." She would have risen, but he put out a hand to hold her where she was.

"There is an old custom. If a man draw a maid from dire danger, he has certain rights—"

For a moment she did not understand; when she did her bruised pride strengthened her to meet his eyes.

"You speak of maids—I am not such."

His indrawn breath made a small sound, but one loud in the silence between them. "So that was the why! You are no farm or tavern wench, are you? So you could not accept what he had done to you. But have you no kinsman to trade for your honor?"

She laughed raggedly. "Marshal, my kinsman had but one wish: that I submit to ancient practices among women so that he would not be shamed before his kind. Having done so I would have been allowed to dwell by sufferance in my own home, being reminded not more than perhaps thrice daily of his great goodness."

"And this you would not do. But with your great hate against him who fathered what you carry—"

"No!" Her hands went to that talisman of Gunnora's. "I have been to the shrine of Gunnora. She has promised me my desire—the child I bear will be mine wholly, taking nothing from *him!*"

"And did she also send you to the Toads?"

Hertha shook her head. "Gunnora guards life. I knew of the Toads from old tales. I went to them in my blindness and they gave me that which I placed in your bed to draw you to them. Also they changed my face in some manner. But—that is no longer so?"

"No. Had I not known your cloak, I should not have known you.

But this thing in my bed— Stay you here and wait. But promise me this, should I return as one under orders, bar the door in my face and keep me here at all costs!"

"I promise."

He went with the light-footed tread of one who had learned to walk softly in strange places because life might well depend upon it. Now that she was alone her mind returned to the matter of what could come to her with the morn. Who would give her refuge—save perhaps the Wise Women of Lethendale. It might be that this marshal would escort her there. Though what did he owe her except such danger as she did not want to think on. But although her thoughts twisted and turned she saw no answer except Lethendale. Perhaps Kuno would someday—no! She would have no plan leading in that path!

Trystan was back holding two sticks such as were used to kindle brazier flames. Gripped between their ends was the pebble she had brought from the Toads' hold. As he reached the fire he hurled that bit of rock into the heart of the blaze.

He might have poured oil upon the flames so fierce was the answer as the pebble fell among the logs. Both shrank back.

"That trap is now set at naught," he observed. "I would not have any other fall into it."

She stiffened, guessing what he thought of her for the setting of that same trap.

"To say I am sorry is only mouthing words, but—"

"To one with such a burden, lady, I can return that I understand. When one is driven by a lash one takes any way to free oneself. And in the end you did not suffer that I be taken."

"Having first thrust you well into the trap! Also—you should have let them take me then as they wished. It would only have been fitting."

"Have done!" He brought his fist down on the seat of the settle beside which he knelt. "Let us make an end to what is past. It is gone. To cling to this wrong or that, keep it festering in mind and

151

heart, is to cripple one. Now, lady," she detected a new formality in his voice, "where do you go, if not to your brother's house? It is not in your mind to return there, I gather."

She fumbled with the talisman. "In that you are right. There is but one place left—the Wise Women of Lethendale. I can beg shelter from them." She wondered if he would offer the escort she had no right to ask, but his next question surprised her.

"Lady, when you came hither, you came by the Old Road over ridge, did you not?"

"That is so. To me it seemed less dangerous than the open highway. It has, by legend, those who sometimes use it, but I deemed those less dangerous than my own kind."

"If you came from that direction you must have passed through Nordendale—what manner of holding is it?"

She had no idea why he wished such knowledge, but she told him what she had seen of that leaderless dale, the handful of people there deep sunk in a lethargy in which they clung to the ruins of what had once been thriving life. He listened eagerly to what she told him.

"You have a seeing eye, lady, and have marked more than most given such a short time to observe. Now listen to me, for this may be a matter of concern to both of us in the future. It is in my mind that Nordendale needs a lord, one to give the people heart, rebuild what man and time have wasted. I have come north seeking a chance to be not just my own man, but to have a holding. I am not like Urre, who was born to a hall and drinks and wenches now to forget what ill tricks fortune plays.

"Who my father was"—he shrugged—"I never heard my mother say. That he was of no common blood, that I knew, though in later years she drudged in a merchant's house before the coming of the invaders for bread to our mouths and clothing for our backs. When I was yet a boy I knew that the only way I might rise was through this"—he touched the hilt of his sword. "The merchant guild welcomed no nameless man, but for a sword and a bow there is always

152

a ready market. So I set about learning the skills of war as thoroughly as any man might. Then came the invasion and I went from Lord to Lord, becoming at last Marshal of Forces. Yet always before me hung the thought that in such a time of upheaval, with the old families being killed out, this was my chance.

"Now there are masterless men in plenty, too restless after years of killing to settle back behind any plough. Some will turn outlaw readily, but with a half dozen of such at my back I can take a dale which lies vacant of rule, such as this Nordendale. The people there need a leader, I am depriving none of lawful inheritance, but will keep the peace and defend it against outlaws—for there will be many such now. There are men here, passing through Grimmerdale, willing to be hired for such a purpose. Enough so I can pick and choose at will."

He paused and she read in his face that this indeed was the great moving wish of his life. When he did not continue she asked a question:

"I can see how a determined man can do this thing. But how will it concern me in any way?"

He looked to her straightly. She did not understand the full meaning of what she saw in his eyes.

"I think we are greatly alike, lady. So much so that we could walk the same road, to profit of both. No, I do not ask an answer now. Tomorrow"—he got to his feet stretching—"no, today, I shall speak to those men I have marked. If they are willing to take liege oath to me, we shall ride to Lethendale, where you may shelter as you wish for a space. It is not far—"

"By horse," she answered in relief, "perhaps two days west."

"Good enough. Then, having left you there, I shall go to Nordendale—and straightway that shall cease to be masterless. Give me, say, threescore days, and I shall come riding again to Lethendale. Then you shall give me your answer as to whether our roads join or no."

"You forget," her hands pressed upon her belly, "I am no maid, nor widow, and yet I carry—"

"Have you not Gunnora's promise upon the subject? The child will be wholly yours. One welcome holds for you both."

She studied his face, determined to make sure if he meant that. What she read there—she caught her breath, her hands rising to her breast, pressing hard upon the talisman.

"Come as you promise to Lethendale," she said in a low voice. "You shall be welcome and have your answer in good seeming."

This last story is the work of John Jakes, who lives in Columbus, Ohio, works in an advertising agency as copy chief, and has for the past two decades written vast quantities of heroic adventure stories, both science fiction and fantasy, for the good of his soul.

Born in Chicago in 1932, John holds a degree from Ohio State University. A tall, heavily-built, youngish man with a graying crewcut and inexhaustible enthusiasm for Sword & Sorcery, John was one of the first to respond to the notion of founding SAGA—with a loud yell of delight, I might add!

Since about 1963, John has been recording the adventures of that splendid, blond-maned, savage warrior, Brak the Barbarian. Brak's world is on a plane parallel to our own (my own private name for it, unsanctioned by its creator, is "Para-Terra"). Many of the Brak the Barbarian adventures appeared first in the Ziff-Davis magazine, *Fantastic*. Beginning with a book aptly titled *Brak the Barbarian* (Avon, 1968), these older adventures, together with brand-new ones, have been incorporated in a series of books. The second volume was *Brak the Barbarian vs. the Sorceress* and the third *Brak the Barbarian vs. the Mark of the Demons*, both published by Paperback Library in 1969. There was no Brak book for 1970—or if there was I must have overlooked it on the newsstands—but in that year John produced a splendid and lively Sword & Sorcery novel called *The Last Magicians*, which he thoughtfully dedicated to his colleagues of SAGA.

I shall not attempt to say how much I enjoyed *The Last Magi-

cians, except to say that, if anything, I think it is even better than Brak. And I am very fond of Brak . . .

John works fully in the Conan tradition and is quite frank about it. On this topic he once said: "That teller of marvelous tales, Robert Howard, did indeed create a giant in whose shadow other 'hero tales' must stand . . . my motive for giving birth to Brak was that there just are not enough stories of this kind to go around. To help fill this dismal gap well or badly—I hope never indifferently—my barbarian with the long yellow braid and the light of the south horizons in his eyes was born."

When he sent me the following story, John Jakes enclosed a brief note with it, which I reproduce here:

"This story is meant to take place immediately after Brak's adventures in 'Devils in the Walls'; thus 'Ghoul's Garden' classifies as the 'latest' in Brak's wanderings—he gets a little further south with each story. Also, some readers have written from time to time that Brak doesn't seem overly interested in girls—to put it politely. I hope 'Ghoul's Garden' helps—if you'll pardon the expression—lay that to rest discreetly."

It certainly should.

Ghoul's Garden

by JOHN JAKES

1

THE DAPPLED woodlands were a refreshing contrast with the sere, poverty-ridden country which the big barbarian had quitted three moons back, having been enslaved, then freed—by dint of his own strength—after facing the demons in Prince Hamur's enchanted palace.

Here there was no thought of the dead woman, the dead slaver, the leopards, the green-slimed treasure. Here, instead, his pony ambled along in the shifting light of a mild sun falling through crimson-leafed trees.

The breeze washed him with its sweetness. Up in a tree a glittering bird inclined its head and rilled at the riding man, who was huge and strong-looking and wore a lion-hide garment around his middle.

The pony loafed down the barely passable track through the woods. The big man rode with rude grace, his long yellow braid bobbing against his back in hoof-rhythm.

The barbarian had worked hard for the lithe little pony with the foam-colored mane. Threshed grain several weeks for a rude-tempered farmer. But suffering the slurs of so-called civilized men was worth it; the pony represented mobility; the big man's chance, again, to ride on. For despite the demons and other terrifying circumstances which he had encountered since his banishment from the high steppes, the wild lands of the north, he was, inevitably, bound to seek his fortune in the warm climes of Khurdisan far southward.

A warm, mellow afternoon. His scars, which sometimes ached in the rain, were healing. His eyes were easy, his mouth relaxed. So when the cry came, round a murky, thicketed bend just ahead, he drew up tight, clutched the rope rein, then let his shoulders slump again.

Some of the quick fire seeped from his eyes. He'd heard a cackle of macabre laughter, no more.

Still—laughter? In the middle of a forest in which he hadn't seen so much as a peasant for several leagues?

The cry came again. Brak the barbarian nudged his pony with his knees. "Wrong," he muttered. "That's a yell of hurt." But uttered, his mind tagged on, by one who squealed easily.

The cry split the wood again.

"Up and look, little one," he said to the pony. It picked up its hoofs, jumping some brambles. The shining bird flew away with a scream. Then Brak heard another sound. A soughing and whipping, as of strong winds through the trees.

The pony trotted around the bend. There, the trees thickened over, so that it grew suddenly chilly, and Brak had trouble making

158

out details of the scene revealed to him. When he did, he hauled back on the pony's rope and boomed a laugh.

A short distance ahead along the track, a man whose gray habit proclaimed him a priest of the cult of Nestoriamus hung upside down in the air, one ankle wrapped round by the end of a supple branch of a great gnarled tree whose bark had a peculiar purplish shine, as of ichor oozing through from the heartwood.

The priest thus caught, dangling and thrashing like a snared animal, had the hem of his inverted robe hanging around his head like a bell. His face was hidden. His squeal sounded again. Something in Brak's middle turned over.

"A coward's wail," he grumbled, and it distressed him no little. He had been occasionally perplexed and even awed by the religious pratings of the disciples of the ecstatic goatherd, Nestoriamus. But he had never met a friar yet—and he'd encountered several—who was not stern stuff. This one yelped and kicked. Well, there were always exceptions. Also, Brak noted, Nestorians wore underdrawers.

In the act of urging his pony onward, he noticed two more things.

Another person was present, frantically trying to tug the Nestorian down from the tree. A woman. Possibly young. She wore a coarse, gaudy skirt and blouse. Green necklaces of stone circled her neck. Her hair flashed deep red in a sunbar, and looked slatternly.

And the tree—nameless gods!

The tree was *breathing*.

A sticky maw opened and shut, opened and shut at the junction where three main branches formed the trunk. The wind-sigh came from no air currents through the woodland but from that sucking, toothless mouth.

And the creeper-like branch that had wrapped itself around the friar's ankle was bending, writhing, flexing—as if to swing the priest over so that the tree could make a meal.

Suddenly cold, Brak kicked the pony hard. He reached back, unslung the broadsword from where he'd lashed it across his muscled back with a length of gut. His fingers broke the loose knot and he had the hilt in his huge-fingered hand. He rode down the dim track noisily, as the confusion at the tree continued.

The woman was young. Another bar of light into which she turned revealed it. And she was much painted. As she spun, she saw help. Letting go of the priest's arm, she screamed like a harpy and gestured.

The priest continued to waul. Here and there on the tree Brak saw shining globular fruits hanging, black skins glowing like waxed ebon—

And the maw opened, shut, opened, shut, noisy as a windstorm.

He reined up. In the gloom he perceived a slash of color. Something ran down the priest's leg from the place where the creeper clutched.

Something that shone in the sunshine. Shone red.

"Stand aside, woman," Brak shouted, off the pony and running. "I'll cut him down."

So saying, he leaned in and raised his broadsword high, double-handing the hilt for a better blow. He felt the impact of the wench's breast, large, soft, as she stumbled out of his way. He smelled her cheap, not unpleasing scent.

The roar of the maw grew louder, it seemed, louder and more angry. From within the bell of the robe hanging down around his head, the priest kept on screaming intermittently. The line of blood reached his knee, trickled on down his thigh toward his drawers.

"*Another arm—!*" That was the wench shrilling. But Brak didn't realize what she meant till a rough, writhing thing lashed, *smack*, across his chest, then crawled—*crawled*—up to his throat in an eye-blink.

The creeper wrapped round and round, and constricted.

Brak's rage came out a growl. He planted his great legs, the yellow braid and the lion tail whipsawing as he tried to wrench free of the tightening creeper. The creeper clutched his neck all the tighter. Fireballs with pointed arms burst inside his head, and there was intense pain.

Unseeing, he hacked down. He felt the broadsword skate off the creeper's rough bark. His eyesockets were afire. Darkness pressed in from the corners of his mind.

Raging, full of red hate, he swung maniacally, chopping the broadsword from the right, from the left, the right—

Abruptly, the creeper cracked.

The maw keened in unholy rage, the windsound sharpening to a shriek. Brak leaped back as two more creepers dropped twitching toward his face. One rasped his cheek but he eluded it. The severed creeper round his throat poured foul pasty brown stuff from its cut end. But it did not release.

The brown odor rose sickeningly. The big barbarian dropped the broadsword and tore at the creeper with both hands, tore and tore, wounding his own flesh with his yellow-thick nails. He couldn't stop. The compulsion to get the awful thing away from him was like a bewitchment.

At last he broke the hold. Beneath its bark the creeper felt alive, muscled. He stamped on it when it fell, then picked it up and threw it away like a still-writhing serpent. Panting, he dove for his broadsword as another creeper, then two, lashed at his shoulder. He dodged away.

"What kind of a hell's tree—?" he half screamed to the girl.

"Witch-apple," she cried back. "The friar and I were traveling together—we walked too close—"

The friar was still howling like one peering into the infernal regions a last time. Strange, unmanly behavior for one of the order, Brak thought again. He wiped his mouth, lowered his head, stared balefully at the dangling priest.

A second creeper had fixed itself round the man's scrawny middle, and slowly, slowly, while the tree-maw roared like the wind, the Nestorian was being drawn up and over to the place where the three mighty branches joined.

Still hurting from the clutch of the creeper on his neck, Brak let the red wrath of the berserker claim him completely. He charged in, hacking and mauling with the sword until he smelled the putrid brown paste dripping from hacked branches.

He severed the creeper round the priest's waist, then the one round his ankle. The man dropped, nearly smashing his brains out on a large stone.

The priest flopped over, his head, balding and horse-jawed, popping out of his tangled robes. Then, on hands and knees, he scuttled away from the demon tree. Brak had a glimpse of moistened eyes turned in fury at the slatternly girl.

"You—slut," the priest panted. "You didn't—" Gulping air. "—act swiftly enough. I—" Gulping, gulping. "—might have died!"

Then he was up, twisting the girl's arm. Over his shoulder he saw Brak glaring. He let go, pale and sullen-faced. The girl cried out.

Maddened by its loss, the witch-apple thrashed its creepers and flailed two, four, six at the big barbarian to seize him from all sides.

Brak jumped high, cut through the nearest one, dodged beneath another—and knew he'd never escape the evil growth using only the iron of his sword. He flung the blade away. It clanged on a rock, making the pony start.

Brak bent, grunted in pain and effort as he locked hands on the stone on which the priest had almost dashed his head open. A creeper slid toward his right foot. He stamped on it. Another reached to twine round his yellow braid. The big barbarian jerked his head aside. Tearing some hair, he got free.

Then he shoved the immensely heavy rock up high over his head and ran two, three, four stumbling steps. His arm muscles hurt from the weight. But he kept going until he could drop the rock down into the tree's maw.

The rock fell out of sight. For a moment all the creepers relaxed, trailed to the ground. Then, abruptly, came the most hideous sound the big barbarian had ever heard.

Deep within itself the tree was roaring and grinding, making a noise of choking, of anguish—

The maw opened out to full width and the witch-apple began to vomit up a geyser of the brown paste streaked with yellow.

Exhausted, Brak hid his eyes behind his forearm and whirled and smashed into the priest and the wench.

"Run! Run fast!"

Somehow he recovered his broadsword. Swinging wide of the track through brambles that raked his legs, he dragged the pony by its rope until he was past the witch-apple. Great slabs of slimy bark were falling from the tree as it shook itself and made that awful sound within its guts. The creepers lashed the ground like whips, hitting so furiously that they broke, oozing brown pasty stuff. The maw was vomiting up brilliant yellow fluid now, thick as molten gold.

Blundering ahead, pushing priest and wench down the track while he pulled his pony, the big barbarian didn't look back more than once.

2

THEY CAMPED together at sunfall. Not exactly willingly; simply because they had been thrown into each other's company. The wood grew quickly dark.

They were in a glade. Brak took eager comfort from the fire he struck with flints and metal which the girl produced from a large, much-patched carry-bag. The barbarian couldn't recall her picking up the bag when they fled the witch-apple, but obviously she had. And she placed great importance on it, too.

His eyes grew amused as the girl replaced the iron and flints, then rummaged among the other items she'd spread out: a little skin wine flacon; a cloth bundle which proved to contain a somewhat mouldy loaf of unleavened bread; various items of clothing and cheap jewelry; and several small stone pots with skin covers. There were pink and scarlet smears all over the pots. The colors matched those of the girl's smeared mouth and cheeks.

A much-painted woman, he mused as the fire warmed his out-stretched hands. Not old, but hard-used by the world. She was hand-some. Had a fine figure. And he rather liked her quick, capable way of moving. As she bent, her blouse fell away from her breasts.

Brak grunted to himself. He had traveled alone a long while. An image of Rhea, the queen he loved, gentled through his mind then. But it did not stay overlong.

"—in here somewhere," she was saying. "This is all in the world I have for belongings." Out came more articles of clothing. Something fell from them, glaring by firelight.

A dagger.

Off in the distance, a loon-like cry rang through the woods. She kept talking:

"I carry a pot of the soothing paste because we often played small towns where there was no leech or cutter. Whenever one of our company was hurt in a play-fight on stage, I became the leech, re-quired to tend and dress—"

"Can't you stop that yammer, woman?"

The unpleasant voice grated across the flames. It stirred a wrath in Brak that he could not explain. The Nestorian sat yonder, his spindly leg thrust out. His wound had clotted. The dried blood looked ugly.

"The girl's trying to find something to tend your hurt, priest," Brak said. "Show a little gratitude. You've done nothing but complain since we left that accursed tree."

The priest's perpetually moist eyes threw back points of firelight. "I need no lessons in deportment from an unlettered—"

"By the gods," said the girl with a sigh. "He *saved* you, Friar Hektor. I couldn't have done it."

Friar Hektor glanced away. "I believe I thanked the outlander back on the road."

Brak grunted. The Nestorian had not, but he said nothing.

"Well, patience," the girl said, hauling out more apparel from the bag. Brak laughed out loud.

She raised her head, the green stones of her necklaces shining against her cleavage. She smiled. It softened the hardness of her, and stirred Brak deep down. Friar Hektor made another querulous sound.

"Here, holy man." Brak tore off a chunk of the mouldy bread, tossed it across the fire. "Nourish yourself." A gesture to the cross hanging from a cord at the priest's waist. The cross was gray stone, with arms of equal length. "Or keep busy speaking with that nameless one all you gray-robes worship."

Friar Hektor couldn't help catching the dislike in Brak's voice. And, in truth, the big barbarian couldn't help himself either. The Nestorian seemed a mean man, soured by the world.

Hektor retorted, "Have a care in what you say about the gods. Blasphemy is—"

"I fear nothing from your god," Brak snarled back.

"Nor from any, I suspect," said the priest with contempt. "It's obvious you worship your own thick arms and that filthy instrument of murder you carry."

Useless to carp back and forth with such a spoiled, twisted specimen, Brak thought. Yet the man's meanness so provoked him that he reached out and stroked the broadsword and said:

"'Tis something real to believe in, anyway. When you ram it down the mouth of some troublemaking fool and see him pour up blood, you know it's worked. I doubt the same can always be said of your god—who, by the way, seemed to be doing a poor job of saving your life back there."

Friar Hektor was visibly shaken by Brak's cruel, joking tone. The last words flushed him with anger. "I have thanked you once, and once is enough for—"

"Oh, bother!"

The friar turned toward the girl. "What's that you say?"

The girl jumped up, a stone pot in her hand. "Surely he has a name. Be gracious enough to use it."

Then she tossed her deep red hair. Rounding the fire, she glanced obliquely at Brak.

"What is your name, anyway?"

He told them, and explained that he was a wanderer, traveling by the most convenient roadways south, toward Khurdisan.

"My name's Shana." Kneeling, she began to apply a pale blue paste to the priest's wound. He winced and complained but she paid no attention, continuing to Brak: "This is hardly a convenient road, is it? This country is so desolate. I hate it. Besides the witch-apples that grow all through here, tales say there are many thieves and brigands who roam these parts. Oh, be still, priest!" she finished.

Friar Hektor ceased his clack, ugly-eyed.

"I've seen no one rich enough to rob," Brak grinned. "Certainly I am not."

Shana smiled back, a warm, softening smile. "Nor I. In truth I only took this route because it's the most direct to Thenngil."

He repeated the name, as a question.

"A province some leagues south," she said. "I have a cousin there. A farmer with a good wife and a brood of young. I—" Her voice broke a moment. "I hope to live with them till I decide what's next for me. I'll work to earn my keep, of course," she added, firmly.

"What's next, you say? Something important is recently over?"

"Our troupe is no more."

"Troupe?"

Hektor said, "She means she was one of a company of traveling players. As I told you before, girl, you're better off out of that business. 'Tis fit only for whores."

"Thank you very much," she replied, "but I've worked the roads ten years now, ever since my breasts grew, and I've never offered myself casually, nor sold myself to any man. Those men that I have —well, that is—there must be—"

After a hesitation she bent to tying off the strip of rag which she was using to bandage the priest's leg. She finished softly:

"There must be a liking."

"What happened to your troupe?" Brak wanted to know. "I have never seen a play-show, if that's what you call them. But I've heard of them."

Shana explained that several towns back the troupe master, one Onselm, had become involved with a woman whose husband returned unexpectedly and, in a duel, slew the actor. "He was our genius. Our teacher, our keeper of the purse. It was he who argued with the locals over the price of our engagements. Without him the troupe lost heart. At the last village, Megaro—" Something sick lay in her eyes then. Some tainted memory that made her shudder. "—we decided to disband, for we all realized we were little good without Onselm. He'd worked the roads forty years and more."

Brak waved a chunk of bread. "How did you two come together, then?"

"We met on the road back there, before the wood," Hektor answered, pushing the girl's hand away as she tried to adjust his bandage. He stood, groaning. He was, Brak saw, a small man. "Since we were going the same way, south, we decided we would be safer together."

Brak tried to hide his continued nasty amusement. Hektor obviously doubted the wisdom of his own decision.

"Your purpose," asked Brak, "being to avoid those thieves and brigands she mentioned?"

"Really, it's true—we have nothing worth stealing," Shana said, opening the flacon. She drank like a man, over her arm.

She wiped the flacon on her skirt and passed it to Brak. He put his lips to it and tasted the pleasing afterscent of hers.

Shana crouched down beside the fire, continuing, "But even

though we're penniless, it's wise to be careful. The woods people have lived so long with plundering and hurting, so the tales say, they do it for the pleasure now, whether there's booty or not. In numbers—"

"Safety," Brak nodded. But he wondered again at the awful, frightened way she eyed the dark trees beyond the ring of light.

The trees whispered in the wind. The night was growing bone-cold. "Where are you bound, friar, besides south?" he asked.

"On a missionary journey." That was that.

Shana helped herself to more wine after Brak passed it back. She offered the flacon to the priest. He raised his hand, as though the offer, like the flacon, was unclean. The girl shrugged, drank a third time, shivered. Brak wondered at that too, until she said:

"Now that we've a little quiet, there is something I must say to you both, in case you want to go on separately."

Hektor scowled. "Something you haven't told me?"

"Y—yes." The wind had flushed her cheeks. "I wanted to but—somehow, I couldn't bring myself—"

"Weakness," muttered the priest. His gaze accused her of causing him more unpleasantness. She pressed her palms against her thighs and kept her head bent as if she were afraid of their faces:

"One of the chief reasons I fled alone, by night, from Megaro town, was that a—a certain man watched us play our last performance there. When it was done, he came to find me. He said"—Again she trembled—"he said he wanted me."

Picking at his teeth, Brak remarked, "Doesn't a woman find it pleasant to be told she's attractive?"

Up came her head, the dark red hair aglitter. There was a hellish fear in her eyes.

"You haven't seen this man."

"Some glutted old satyr, no doubt," Hektor sniffed. "Offering you a few dinshas for—"

"No. He told me"—Her hands pressed white on her legs—"he told me he would offer me nothing. That he need offer me nothing because he was a wizard."

In the cooling night the lonely bird sounded again. Brak's spine crawled without him willing it. He said nothing. Shana went on:

"He called himself Pom."

Hektor snorted. "No fancy thaumaturgical titles?"

Shana stared into the fire as if staring at the unspeakable. Her voice was barely audible:

"Just Pom. A man no taller than"—She indicated her breasts—"here. With a curious child's body, thin and odd, as though it had all been broken in the past and mended together wrong. Or never put together right in the first place. But his head was this large." Her hands spread apart. "With not a hair on it, giving him the look of some ghastly little boy. His eyes—you have never seen such eyes—round and milky-gray. Huge." Suddenly, watching the fire, she bowed her head and bit the back of her hand.

Even Hektor found nothing to say, for the fear in the glade was like a poison. Presently Shana glanced up again. She said:

"There's little more to tell, except that I slipped away from him. He seemed a poor man, with a threadbare robe. But he said wizards did not need fine apparel, for they controlled a secret, more beautiful world. He had a black pony, I remember. Lashed to its back was an old leathern trunk. Not large, just very old. He said that if I would lay with him, he'd open the trunk and show me mystical things. A garden where the air smelled of balm, and it was ever twilight, and golden metal birds sang in trees beside a pool full of diamonds—"

She stared at Brak, as if seeking protection. "He described it as beautiful and yet, somehow, I knew it was—an evil place."

Quickly she drank again.

Friar Hektor began to finger his stone cross and eye the surrounding dark. Brak knew that without a doubt they were in the company of a coward.

"Well," he said, as lightly as he could, "I'm bound south too. We'll all go together for a ways, and damn the wizard." A moment later, "You don't think he followed you, do you?"

Shana's eyes were empty. "I have no reason to think he did. Except—the lust in him—so crippled, wanting a whole woman so badly—I suppose it's possible that he might—"

"Well," Brak said again, shrugging, "I've this to protect us." He crouched down near the slowly dying fire and slapped his broadsword. Then he pointed to Hektor. "And our holy man has his little cross, and that should pull us through. Anyway, your wizard was probably just some sickly beggar ragging you with scare tales of an empty trunk."

Shana looked at Brak the barbarian once more, and tried to believe.

"Yes, you could be right. Yes, I'm glad you said that. Now I can sleep. We'll travel on together."

Somehow she found yet another item—a frowzy sleeping rug—inside the bag. She rolled up in it, giving Brak one final, thankful glance. He thought briefly of her body beneath her cheap, bright clothes, then decided this was the wrong time. With the sword iron against his belly he settled down.

Friar Hektor was mumbling some incantation or other to his Nameless God. That kept Brak awake awhile, annoyed. Finally the priest quieted, as did the flames. Silence deepened in the glade.

Brak turned this way, that, left side, right side, left again. He heard similar restless noises from Shana. But at last these too ceased. He fell into a thin, uneasy slumber.

He had a dream.

He was lying rigid, on his back, unmoving and unable to move, staring up through moonfired treetops at a great beast, a black horse, thundering down the sky in silence with a stunted rider on its back.

The hoofs of the beast slashed the air but it made no sound in its passing, only trailed thin streams of fire from its nostrils. It loomed larger than the moon a moment, then passed on into the silvered clouds, southward.

Dazed, Brak sat up. He clutched his sword and nicked himself on the cutting edge. He said an oath and sucked his finger. Then, almost afraid of what he would see, he raised his eyes—

And saw the same moondrenched treetops.

Had he dreamed? *Had* he?

In the silvered sky, two faint parallel trails, like pink vapor, seemed to be vanishing. The cold night air had a sulphurous stench, as though the world had opened and belched forth some of its evil; evil that now lingered to taint, to promise—unspeakable things.

He slept badly the rest of the night.

3

MORNING BROUGHT gloom, and rain.

Thunder smote the forest. Long blue streaks of lightning crisscrossed the sky. The downpour continued an inordinately long time, during which Brak was forced to squat scowling in the cover of the trees, rain dripping off his matted yellow brows. His eyes strayed now and then to Shana. She was as disgusted as he by Friar Hektor's constant complainings.

Eventually the rain let off to a drizzle. They agreed to resume their journey.

Friar Hektor demanded that he be allowed to ride Brak's pony. The barbarian gave him a hand up, rougher than necessary, and took pleasure when the priest winced.

"I meant to offer you the animal," Brak said. He turned his back and set off down the track, yellow braid swinging.

The rain continued intermittently, and the forest gradually thinned. The sky grew dark again, an early nightfall because of the fast-flying clouds that only occasionally split to shine silver from the hidden sun. Brak stopped slogging along the muddy track and held up a hand, ears all sharp.

"A strange sound—" he began.

Shana came up beside him, lugging her carry-bag over her shoulder. Her old, worn slipper skidded on a mud-slimed, half-buried rock. She crashed against Brak, exclaiming in embarrassment.

With her free hand she pushed back her limp, wet hair. For a moment their eyes held. Then the big barbarian turned away again. He wasn't easy in such situations, and he felt unmanned by what he was sure the girl saw in his eyes: naked admission of his feelings.

"We're coming to a river," Friar Hektor said as Brak's pony plopped up behind them. "Anyone can hear that."

The barbarian stifled a retort and, as he did, Shana put in, "From the noise it's running fast. Probably because of the rain. We won't cross tonight, I'll wager."

Somehow Brak felt uneasy about that. He signed them forward and in a short time they emerged in lowering night on a weedy bank.

The river was not wide. But it ran at furious speed over treacherous-looking rocks directly in front of them. Dark had all but fallen. Brak perceived details but dimly.

Foams and whorls of swift white water barred their path. On the far side he glimpsed the barest suggestion of the track continuing up among the boulders into more rugged terrain.

Brak crouched, tracing a forefinger in the mud. He dipped the finger down into an indentation.

"There's the track of a hoof here. More than one. But how many passed here earlier, and whether they went across or turned back, I can't tell. It could be one rider, it could be several."

He slashed the drizzle off his forehead. "If it weren't so cursed dark—"

But cursing was no use. The hoof prints were lost. It grew blacker moment by moment. The wind was picking up, chilling him deep.

He raised his head, stared out across the water that boiled with faint luminescence. "Obviously, since the track comes down to here, there's a ford somewhere about. But at night—"

"If you think I intend to risk myself on such a chancy crossing when we've no light, you're mistaken," Friar Hektor exclaimed.

Brak stood up, wiped his free hand on the lion-skin at his waist. He took a harder grip on the hilt of his broadsword. The iron blade was resting across one brawny shoulder, point aimed behind him.

"We won't subject your noble person to such hazards, priest. We'll make camp on this side and cross with the light."

"We'll camp if we can find a dry place," Shana said wearily.

"Up the bank—" Brak began, swinging that way.

And saw, for the first time, a human figure silhouetted against a rectangle of deep, smudgy orange, not far to his left down the riverside.

With a start he realized it was a man. The man was standing in a cottage doorway with firelight behind him. A man of good physical size, too. Well set up, with a large head topped by curly hair. The man raised his hand and hallooed:

"Travelers?"

"Aye," Brak shouted back. "Travelers seeking shelter from the rain."

"Come this way, my house is yours."

Friar Hektor hissed through his teeth. "The girl spoke of cruel men in these wild parts. Foresters who prey upon—"

Brak's vile oath shut the priest up. "I'm sick of your carping and your damn dissatisfaction, priest. That's a big man yonder, but I see no more than one of him, and I'm tired and hungry, and I'll trade the risks for a chance at his fire. You may be terrified of him but I'm not. Sit out here in safety and misery all night if it pleases you, but in case it does, haul your shanks off my pony. He deserves shelter in the lee of the house."

With that, Brak grabbed the pony's rein and jerked.

Friar Hektor was forced to slide quickly to the ground before being dumped off by the pony's sudden forward motion. For a moment Hektor's face was lit by the dim glare from the cottage.

The Nestorian barely stood to Brak's neck. In the small man's upturned eyes the barbarian saw the sad, foolish loathing of the small for the larger. With his broadsword over his shoulder and his pony rope in the other hand, he plodded toward the cottage.

He was wary; wary but not alarmed. Yet there was something, *something*, prickling uneasily at the back of his mind—

"That's sensible talk at last," Shana said as she fell in step beside him. Friar Hektor resumed his grumbling. But he followed.

"Welcome, welcome," the tall man said as they approached. He stepped back into the small, rude house, which had a reed roof. Up there smoke crawled from a pot set among the reeds.

The man turned sidewise. Firelight fell athwart his face. Something about that face made Brak's mind prickle even more.

The man was young, with broad shoulders, a small waist, and a handsome, tanned face. A man of strength, vigor; a man open to the weather. Nothing there of which to be suspicious. Yet Brak didn't like him.

He felt the dislike even more strongly when the man smiled at Shana with unhidden interest. The man did pause long enough to point around the cottage corner and say to the barbarian, "There's a bale of woods grass somewhere back there. The pony can feed."

Then he stepped even farther back inside, executing a half bow. Decidedly odd behavior for one living so far apart from others, Brak thought. Even he, an unlettered offspring of the wild northern lands, had been among civilized peoples long enough to know that.

The man touched Shana's arm as she passed inside. He smiled, a wide, white, perfect smile of charm and ease.

"Come in, please, and get yourselves warm and dry. My name's Yan. I'm a woodcutter. I see few strangers. I'm glad of the company."

Brak located the woods grass bale and left the pony tied and chomping. He thought he heard another animal stirring out in the weeds where the rain pattered, but saw nothing, so he headed back inside. His teeth were chattering from the cold. He was more tired than he had imagined. Something ran around in his head, a peculiar thought—

A woodcutter, a woodcutter.

And to whom does he sell his wood, leagues from anyone or anything?

The absence of rain and the sudden curl of fire-warmth against his skin made him abandon the bothersome thought. He slung down his broadsword as Friar Hektor made for the only stool in the one-room house. There were few other furnishings: a rude table, a pallet of blankets laid upon straw; an empty blackened kettle hanging from an iron prong beside the fireplace. Yan the woodcutter seemed to have no store of clothing, not even any personal belongings. There were cobwebbings up in the ceiling corners. Brak watched a fat yellow-black spider crawling in its web, then glanced back as Yan spoke to the priest in a courteous tone:

"I believe the lady has first right to sit, father. Would you be so good—?"

Grumbling, Hektor got up. With a little smile that hid her weariness, Shana thanked Yan and sat down. She kicked off her slippers and toasted the bottoms of her dirty feet.

Yan bustled around, drawing the table near her while Brak stood like a rock, watching Shana's grateful expression and the way the woodcutter's dark eyes kept returning to her face.

"Here—wine—cheese—I eat a simple meal at night, but you're all welcome to finish it. There is still plenty, I think."

Friar Hektor extended his hand. "Pass the wine."

Yan did, without so much as a murmur. Something smelled all wrong to Brak.

Perhaps it was only his simple mind. Or perhaps it was another feeling he hated to admit—

Shana was hugging her knees now, feet drawn up on the stool's

175

rung. Yan held out a slab of cheese. She accepted with perfect pleasure.

Brak had seldom seen such a handsome fellow as the woodcutter. He couldn't help disliking the way Shana seemed taken with him.

"Tell me who you are and where you're bound," Yan said as he seated himself on the hearthstone. He wore tight trousers, woodsman's boots, a tunic over a coarse shirt. He seemed elegant of speech for a man who lived far apart from cities.

"My name's Shana. I was part of a traveling troupe—" And she was launched into an explanation of her decision to journey to the farm of her cousin. She mentioned the unwelcome attentions of a man as having contributed to her plan, but she said nothing about a wizard, nor named him. Brak thought he recognized the fear in her eyes again, but just a flicker. She was fighting to conceal it.

Then, a moment later:

She's trying to conceal it so he'll not think her simple and foolish.

Brak felt hot, wrathful. This tough, capable young woman had attracted him more than he cared to admit. He disliked Yan's attentive stare more and more each moment. He felt cloddish in the man's presence.

Suddenly Yan glanced up, his eyes keen as he looked at the big barbarian.

"And you? The lion skin marks you some kind of outlander."

"Called Brak, and bound south." He reached for cheese, unwilling and unable to say more.

"Are you quite warm enough?" Yan inquired of Shana.

"Yes, thank you. The fire's very pleasant."

"If there's anything here to make you more comfortable—" Yan gestured to take in the room. Why did it look so unused? So dusty in the corners? The rain pattered softly, steadily, on the reed roof.

"No, you're most kind," Shana smiled. Gods, how Brak hated this handsome young buck of a sudden.

He was struggling for something to say when he heard a noise outside. The quick, fearful whinny of his pony.

176

Yan looked around, sharply. Brak's belly went tight as the pony started stamping. He left his broadsword leaning against the wall and went outside, catching the pony's head rope just as the animal trotted past the front of the cottage, running away.

Brak tugged. The pony quieted a little. The barbarian rubbed his hand up and down the warm muzzle, talking soothing nonsense.

The pony let its head down and stood still. Brak blinked in the rain. He heard another noise from the rear of the little house.

Something compelled him to quiet. He edged round the cottage corner and slid along the wall until he could make out a shape looming in the weeds—

Brak crouched. A moment later he let out his breath. His reaction had been unwarranted. What stood there was nothing more than a horse. A horse of good size, true, and powerful-looking. But nothing uncommon. He took another step forward, his hardened soles sliding in mud.

The horse tossed its head back and snapped at him.

Brak stopped. He stared at the beast a long moment. Black, it was. Black as the raining night.

Then, as the barbarian's eyes grew more accustomed to the dark, he noted something bulking from the horse's back. He edged a step closer.

The horse tossed its long, tangled mane. A vicious animal. Brak made a sound in his throat, a primitive sound, a sound of threat. Somehow the beast understood, and remained still. Brak recognized the shape jutting up from the horse's back. It was a trunk, strapped in place as if the horse's owner were ready for a swift departure. Not a large trunk, but very old, battered at the corners. A leathern trunk—

"He said if I would lay with him, he'd open the trunk and show me mystical things. A garden where the air smelled of balm, and it was ever twilight—"

Now there was a horror on Brak, the horror of the unknown half glimpsed, and he turned and bolted back to the door of the cottage.

The door was still open. He checked in the dark as the bile of fear rose up in his throat.

Seated against the wall, Friar Hektor had fallen into a doze. Shana perched on her stool by the fire. Between the girl and the doorway Yan the woodsman was reaching for another slab of cheese, his teeth white in a smile, his curly black hair shining. Brak saw Shana's strong, pretty face as through a gauzy curtain—

He saw it through the flesh of Yan's outreaching hand.

The woodsman's hand drew back, carrying a piece of cheese. The barbarian cursed himself for leaving his broadsword inside. So he chose surprise, moving fast, leaping inside the door and to one side, reaching downward.

Yan didn't miss the significance of Brak's outstretched hand. Some of the handsomeness left his face.

"Is there something amiss?"

"Much," Brak growled, broadsword hilt in his grasp. "I don't yet know what, but it's something foul as—"

Crystal-white fire leaped from Yan's hand to the sword. The cottage rang with a sound like a great bell. Brak's head vibrated with pain.

Touched by the fire, the broadsword flew across the room and fell, clattering.

4

BRAK SEIZED THE rude table, hurled it aside so he could get to Yan. The woodsman's handsome face became strangely distorted. His dark eyes glared. Through Yan's tunic the big barbarian saw the cottage wall in clear detail.

"Shana! Out the door!" Brak yelled as he lunged, hands open, fingers ready for Yan's throat.

178

The woodsman backed off a step, made another mesmeric pass in the air. A sheet of crystal-white fire blazed up in front of Brak's eyes, hiding everything, and the thunderous bell-like sound pealed inside his head.

The fire seemed to reach inside Brak's brains and broil them. His huge legs turned weak. He collapsed, twitching, on the floor, drool running out of his mouth. Pain was singing in every fiber of him.

When he jammed his palms on the rude plank floor and tried to push up, he was swept with overwhelming nausea and more pain. He could barely keep his eyes open. He had a bleary, sideways view of the room. Through Yan's boots he saw hearth-flames.

The flash of enchanted fire had roused the Nestorian. Mumbling and quavering, Hektor tottered to his feet.

"I smell devils here—the influence of Yob-Haggoth—" His fingers struggled for a grip on the stone cross hanging at his waist.

Yan made a sound of utter hate, leaped and tore at the cross. The cord hanging from Hektor's waist snapped. Shana shrieked as Yan spun and flung the cross into the fire.

A thunderclap, a boil of intense light—the sound and glare smote Brak like a blow. He flopped over on his back, wondering whether he was dying. Somewhere, distantly, he heard a voice—Shana's—now edged with terror and knowing:

"You—you aren't as you seem. You are someone—"

Her words choked off. Brak rolled over on his belly in time to see the woodsman seize the girl by both shoulders.

"Aye," Yan whispered, staring at her with inhumanly bright eyes. "Aye, it's all illusion here. But now I'll show you what I wanted you to see, from that moment I caught sight of you behind the rushlights on the stage in the square."

As Yan spoke, his voice changed, rose up a scale to a ghoulish, scraping squeal, almost childlike, yet with an ugly undertone. Yan's body began to waver, as though glimpsed through a fall of water. Some smoky shape was forming behind it. *Within* it.

In his weakened, pain-wracked state, Brak knew the reality of his suspicions then. Knew the truth as Yan flung Shana down so hard that she struck her head on the corner of the overturned table.

Yan dashed to the door. He grew dimmer, more insubstantial with each step. Rain slashed his face as he turned his head, looked back into the cottage. Trying to rise, unable, Brak saw a second head, a second face materialize—

Brak blinked against the pain pulsing through him. When his eyes came open, he glimpsed a small, shriveled body crouched in the door in a curiously broken posture. The apparition wore a plain, threadbare robe. Brak saw a huge hairless head, a delicate nose, a tiny mouth. And immense protruding milky-gray eyes staring and staring at Shana, as though she were naked.

Then Pom the wizard vanished in the rain.

5

"UP," Brak mouthed between his teeth.

He heard Friar Hektor whimpering. He managed to push to all fours, started crawling to his fallen broadsword. He knew, in full horror, the depth of Pom's lust; lust that had driven the wizard to speed ahead of them—that steed in the sky, it had been no dream— and set his snare of illusion.

Brak seemed to be crawling up a great plain at a steep angle. Each movement required immense effort. He stretched out his right hand. The fingers trembled. He closed the fingers around the hilt of his fallen blade—

A yell of pure bestial agony tore out of his mouth.

The broadsword blazed with heat. He tore his hand away, half growling, half whimpering. Pom had enchanted the iron with his crystal fire. Pom had made the blade impossible to wield. Brak lay dazed, helpless a moment—

Footfalls.

The hem of a robe swished past Brak's line of vision. The wizard reappeared before the hearth.

Shana was just beginning to rouse. Tears of terror streaked her cheeks. She recognized her surroundings, tried to struggle up. Pom laid a slippered foot on her neck and held her down while he wrestled his old leathern trunk to the ground.

He was speaking as he tore at the rope ties that held the lid in place, speaking in a childish, demented squeak:

"—told you little of myself, I think. Well, I was born in a dark, wet place under the earth. My mother was a tavern whore. My father was a wizard of some skill, but one—" *Crash,* the trunk lid went back. Those immense milky-gray eyes stood forth from his head, sick with desire. "—one who offended many a fearsome god. For that reason I was born as you see me. Crippled. Cursed. No woman will touch me unless I make her touch me, by surrounding her with the one great magic my father had among his effects at the time of his death."

Out of Brak's vision, Friar Hektor cried, "What kind of debased creature are you? If you've the powers of a thaumaturge as you say, why must you behave like a common clod bent on—on rape?"

"Ah, there's the catch, priest." Pom's tiny blue-veined hands dipped out of sight in the open trunk. For a moment his moist eyes reflected a curious agony. "I am but half a wizard. Even my spell-making powers are cursed and bent crooked like my body. When I tricked you, made you see the woodsman—that was a spell, yes." Pom licked his lips, turned to stare at Shana again. "But I cannot hold the spell when I love a woman." His mouth wrenched. "So I must have a proper setting, you see. A proper enchantment. I've wandered the world a hundred years and more—" Hektor gasped. "—chained in this broken flesh, the mark of the curses laid on my father, and the liquorish heat of my mother's lusts driving me on."

The wizard's eyes glared with hate. "She loved her work, she did. A whore of uncontrollable passions." And then his voice became softer, with an evil sibilance, as he looked yet another time at Shana's body. "We are none of us without flaws, y'see. Not even magicians."

And he whirled his fists up from the trunk, his fingers full of a big, dark silk that seemed to blow and billow out in all directions.

With a snap Pom spread the silk, let it settle to the floor beside the trunk. Brak tried to rise again. He was getting a little of his strength back. Pom cast him a wary glance but didn't seem overly alarmed.

Pom crouched down. He knotted one tiny hand in Shana's deep red hair and pulled her head back.

"No woman I've seen in a year has fired me as you have, my girl. You've the smell of the slut on you. Perhaps that's what excites me." Then, like a carrion-creature, he swooped his mouth on hers.

Shana shrieked. The cry was muffled behind the kiss. Pom broke away. Struggling, he pushed his forearms beneath her, lifted her.

Sweat popped out on his smooth, bulging forehead. His breath came hard as he took a labored step toward the silk lying on the floor. "In my father's garden perhaps you'll find yourself bemused enough to submit. Yes, I rather think you will." With a step, he was standing on the edge of the silk.

Instantly he, and Shana in his arms, were gone.

Friar Hektor crab-stepped toward the curiously patterned piece of cloth. His horse-jaw hanging down in horror-struck amazement, the Nestorian put one sandal on the silk.

"Don't touch it!" Brak shouted. "There's some power in it that transports—"

Too late. The priest had both feet on the silk square. He vanished.

6

A DREADFUL stillness enveloped the cottage. It was broken only by tiny sounds: the fragrant fireplace popping, rain blowing in the open doorway and pattering on the floor, the wind of night snapping the silk where it lay, horror creaking inside Brak's head.

After a long moment he was able to stand. He tottered toward the silk, almost fell upon it, righted himself with a yelp of alarm. Then, carefully, he hunkered and studied the intricate patterning of the material.

It had an order, a design, after all. The basic ground color was a blackish green. Into this were worked shapes both regular and otherwise, the former being created by lines that ran in from the edges of the silk and intersected one another. The irregular shapes had no clear pattern, were merely positioned here and there.

Of a sudden the barbarian understood. He was staring down at the plan of some sort of garden. The dividing lines were hedges, the irregular shapes pools and grottos.

As he stared at the silk, it seemed that he heard a faint, faraway singing, as of a woman's voice, very sweet, very beguiling. His backbone crawled.

A garden. A flat garden spread before him as if he were a god. As he stared, he thought he saw tiny motes within the strands of silk, two motes in one place, a single mote in another—

Pom and Shana. Hektor.

Alive in a garden of silk.

Despite his terror, he knew what must be done. He started for the broadsword again, found it still searing to the touch. A weapon. A weapon! He could not essay it without one—

183

His eye fell on Shana's carry-bag lumped in a corner.

He pawed through it like a madman until he found the dagger he'd seen in the wood. He thrust the blade into the lion hide at his waist. Then, wobbling but erect, he stumbled to the edge of the silk.

He swallowed, his palms cold-slick with fear. He took a final look at the dying fire and stepped on the cloth.

Singing and dark engulfed him.

7

OVERHEAD STRETCHED a sky of pink and amber broken by long, sculptured clouds of pearl gray. Brak saw the twilight sky above the trimmed top of a hedge that was half a head taller than he. In the distance someone was singing—that seductive, unearthly voice.

Like the hedges that boxed him round, the grass beneath his feet had a glossy blackness in the subtly poisonous light. The garden was a somber, beautiful place. Yet it sickened him in a way he could not explain.

His head filled with a delicious scent that had a subtle, sensuous tinge. Behind him he heard a metallic plashing.

He turned, muscles loosening a little, and without even thinking, he went into the old, wary half-crouch of the steppe stalker. There was something animal about the baleful eyes, the ready hands finally draining of their pain, the barbaric lion tail and yellow braid hanging down.

The plashing came from a fountain beside a tile-edged pool. The water pouring from the fountain fell in silver droplets. Shana's words came echoing:

"—and it was ever twilight, and golden metal birds sang beside a pool full of diamonds."

184

The silvery water did indeed resemble diamonds falling and drifting. A fish swam into view close to the surface, slithery and graceful. The fish regarded Brak with a multicolored faceted eye, then dove away deep.

Brak began to grunt under his breath, the hate-chant of the hunter. He seemed boxed round by the hedge. But a circuit of the pool showed him a narrow opening.

He eased the dagger into his right hand and slid through sideways. He found himself in another, almost identical area, bordered by hedges. Here, though, a number of trees grew. On a low branch sat one of the golden metal birds, a thing of loveliness that cooed and cooed.

The bird's folded wings reflected the pink and amber of the sky. Listening to the faraway singing, Brak grew drowsy. The woman's voice teased, beckoned, seduced, so that, for a warm, languorous moment, he could only think of one thing—holding a woman in his arms.

Then he remembered Shana's plight. His lips skinned back, ugly again, and he edged past the first of the trees.

Large, opalescent fruits hung from the branches. Brak's belly growled. He plucked down one of the fruits.

It had a soft, yielding skin, and nearly filled his fist. He had the fruit halfway to his mouth when caution checked him.

Instead of eating, he closed his left hand and squeezed.

A thick, cloying perfume rose from the syrupy juice that ran out of the pulp and down his wrist. In the mashed mess in his palm there was suddenly a black worm crawling, a worm twice as long as his middle finger.

The barbarian flung the pulp and worm away. He wiped his hand on the lion hide, as if he'd touched something that was filthy beyond reckoning.

Another opening in the hedge admitted him to still one more boxed-in place, and for some time he went on like this through hedged rooms open to the soft, dully lighted sky.

He was beginning to grow frustrated, angry, when he heard voices.

The enchanted singing receded a little. Brak bellied down in the long black grass. He crept toward a dimly seen opening in the hedge. Through it the voices drifted.

Peering round, he saw an open place where the sward ran up a gentle hill. On its summit sat a white-pillared building much like a miniature temple. In the open interior, through which the breeze blew, a lamp flickered. On the shallow steps leading up to the structure stood the wizard Pom, Friar Hektor beside him.

Pom's huge hairless head gleamed in the perpetual twilight. As did his protruding eyes. He seemed composed, turning his head this way and that, slowly, to study his garden.

"I glanced away but a moment," Brak heard the wizard say. "When I looked back, she'd scuttled off."

"You'll never find her," Hektor told him. He sounded craven.

"Ah, you think not? Of course I will. This is my province. I know every nook of it. The girl hiding will make the game all the more tasty. In fact, I'm not certain but what I wanted her to flee, elude me for a while, just for the joy of the chase."

Slowly Pom turned to regard the Nestorian. The priest, Brak realized, was barely able to control his fright; he was shaking.

"That way"—Pom's voice whispered on the wind above the singing —"when I catch her and lay her bare on the sward, the taking will be all the more delicious." His odd, crookedly put-together body seemed to quiver faintly. He studied the garden.

Friar Hektor hesitated a moment. Then he plucked at Pom's poor robe.

The wizard spun to him, glaring.

"I'll help," the Friar said.

"What do you mean?"

"I'll help search. I'll assist you in every way."

Pom pulled from the holy man's hand distastefully. His little mouth pursed up with cruel joy. "I thought you disciples of the Nameless God were strong, pure men."

"I am my own man. I"—Hektor licked his lips—"I want to live. How I got to this devil's place I don't know, but if I help you, I—I want a bargain. Return me to—wherever we came from. The real world. My life in return for my help." He clutched again. "Bargain, wizard?"

The bile of disgust climbed Brak's throat at the spectacle of the priest bargaining away his last shred of honor. But then, it wasn't so surprising, given Hektor's earlier behavior.

Pom brought his robe to his lips, as if to brush away a speck. He regarded the sky. Within the little white temple the lamp guttered in the wind.

"I will decide," Pom said.

Hektor swallowed, his throat-apple bobbing. "Not now? You won't tell me now?"

"No. You are a despicable man. I prefer a little amusement with you. I'll let you help in the hunt. Perhaps I'll even permit you to watch while the wench and I sport. Then I'll decide whether to return you, or kill you as I planned." Pom's wet eyes were amber and pink in the twilight. "Slowly, priest. Slowly, with exquisite hurt you cannot conceive until you experience it."

Friar Hektor backed down a step. "Madman. Madman."

Pom smiled. "Ah, indeed. But isn't it to be expected of a crippled bastard child cursed from birth? And remember, priest—this is my father's garden. In it you take my terms or you take none at all."

Hektor searched the hill, the sky, the hedges for a means of escape. There was none. His shoulders slumped pathetically. "I've no choice. Shall we search?"

Pom chuckled. "You're a filthy, reprehensible specimen indeed. But somehow I do enjoy you. Yes, we shall. First, though, I prefer to clean my hands and anoint myself so that I'm acceptable when we find her. Wait here."

So saying, the wizard turned and hitched his way up the steps.

He vanished into the temple, a crippled wraith that seemed ready to topple over at any moment because of the outsized weight of its head.

Brak listened. Ever the distant singing. The coo-coo of a golden bird in a tree somewhere. But nary a sound to indicate where Shana might be hiding in terror.

The barbarian felt his own kind of fear, a controlled fear. Unless he was wary, he'd never locate her. How they would escape from this place he didn't know. But he put that greater problem away in order to solve the first: finding the girl.

Presently Pom reappeared from within the temple. He signed to Hektor and the two moved down the hill. They disappeared into an opening in the hedgerows to Brak's left.

The big barbarian took a firmer grip on the dagger, rose and crept after them in a crouch.

He turned into the room of hedge into which they'd vanished. It was very dark. He proceeded cautiously, unable to see the next opening. Somewhere he heard their footfalls. He moved in that direction.

He blundered into the tree without seeing it. Suddenly there was a flash of gold high up over his head against the sky. Disturbed, the metal bird spread its glittering wings. Its coo changed to a caw of rage.

Talons extended as it dropped down to Brak's face. The talons slashed.

Brak whipped his head aside in time to keep his eye from being put out. The talons scored a strike on his forehead, opening a wound that leaked blood into his eyebrows as the barbarian leaped back.

The roused bird circled, climbed, dived again, sharp golden beak driving for Brak's face.

He slashed his dagger hand up across from the right. The dagger point clanged harmlessly off the bird's wing. But the force of Brak's fist drove the bird aside. It seemed to flounder in the air a moment. Then its wings began beating strong again.

188

The bird shrilled and rilled, enraged. The noise carried. Pom exclaimed. There was much thrashing in the hedges.

Almost swifter than sight could follow, the bird shot up against the sky. Brak saw something that horrified him anew: a fat droplet oozing between the tips of the bird's upper and lower beak. A droplet secreted and hanging there—

A poison.

Poison for him.

Down streaked the bird, that black jewel glistening at the tip of the beak. Brak jumped two steps to the side. The bird wheeled and planed out level, coming for his face.

The knife was useless in Brak's hand. He jammed it between his teeth, whipped up both hands and caught the bird's body. He stopped the beak but a hand's width in front of his face.

The bird beat its metal wings. Its talons raked Brak's hands bloody. The bird tried to wrench its head around to peck its poison drop into his thumb. But the barbarian held it off, his strength against its slippery, raking fury.

The beak quested around again, poking viciously. Brak slid his fingers up around the bird's neck, closed them there. He slid his other hand up to follow.

The bird drew its head back for a death-peck. Brak's temples beat with fear. He had but an instant—

Constricting both hands, he wrung the metal bird's neck. Twisted its head awry, tore it off—

Head separated from body. Golden wires hung between. There was a flash of whiteness, a billow of smoke, and Brak felt his face burned raw.

He shrieked like a wounded beast. Blinded, he flung the remains away. His entire face felt seared. The tangled wreckage of the bird dropped on the sward, glowing, molten, bubbling. The head with the glaring eye and the glistening drop in the beak dissolved into little liquid gold rivers that ran out through the black grass.

The knife fell from Brak's teeth. He made bestial sounds in his hroat. His whole face was afire. As he stood there trying to press away the pain, there was a gurgling yell, and scrawny hands attacked his neck from behind.

A knee jolted the small of his back. Taken by surprise, he was driven forward. He crashed face first across the tiled coping of a pool.

The frantic, wordless panting of Friar Hektor became a bubbling roar in Brak's ears as the holy man, with demented strength, thrust the barbarian's head under the water and held it there.

Silver danced in front of Brak's eyes. He tried to reach over his shoulder, grapple at the priest, but somehow the angle was wrong. The silver flakes before his eyes began to darken.

Water filled his nostrils, stung his burned face. Head completely submerged, he didn't dare breathe. His lungs began to pulse with pain.

Friar Hektor couldn't be all that strong. No, that was impossible. But then Brak knew otherwise: for the cowardly priest was bent on saving his own life by taking Brak's, and such men had the power of many.

Hektor's knee ground harder against his backbone.

The barbarian's mind began to shimmer with a peculiar darkness. He knew he hadn't much longer to breathe, to live—

That thought gave him the will to fight the death-lethargy. He gathered all the power left in him, heaved upward—

Hektor fell off into the grass, caterwauling, *"Pom? Wizard? Where are you? Where have you gone? See, I've felled the outlander. Now you must help—!"*

Like one crazed, Brak went scrambling for the dagger he'd dropped. He knew approximately where it was, and he fought forward through the black grass, hands slashing and beating the sward. Friar Hektor was up. He leaped on Brak's back from behind.

Hektor's fingers dug into Brak's eyesockets. They pressed deep. Suddenly Brak touched metal. He closed his fist on the dagger hilt, aimed the point over his shoulder, hurled his fist up and back as Hektor's thumbs pressured his eyeballs into awful agony—

Friar Hektor choked. The sound was long and ugly. Then something warm splashed the barbarian's spine.

The pressure left his eyes. He crawled away, rolled over, squinted half-blind—

Blood. That was blood on his back. It poured from the place where the knife had impaled Hektor's throat.

The Nestorian was stretched up on tiptoes. His hands were uplifted to the pink and amber sky. His face was awful to behold.

"Help me," he cried. "*Help me.*"

No answer came from the god he'd forsaken; only the faraway voice of the woman singing of wicked pleasure. Gazing at perdition in the twilight clouds, Friar Hektor toppled forward. His fall jammed the dagger deeper into his neck. The point protruded from the back of his head, just below his fringe of hair.

A terrible wrath was upon Brak the barbarian. He lumbered over and kicked the Nestorian's twitching corpse so hard that it rolled to the pool and tumbled in. By the uncertain light Brak saw a dirty, skinny ankle sinking beneath the silvered surface. He raised his face to the sky and bayed like a victorious animal.

As the sound died away, he heard another—

Shana's scream.

Brak plunged his hands into the pool, seized the body, tore the dagger out of its throat by main force. Then he ran—crashed—through the hedge-rooms, back toward the open place from which the screaming rose.

His foot slipped as he emerged into the open area around the little white temple. On the shallow steps he saw Shana, fallen, Pom with her, spittle running from the corner of his mouth.

The girl's arms were scratched, and her legs as well. There was little left of her coarse skirt. Apparently Pom had torn it away. The wizard was bending over her, fighting her, pawing her blouse, ripping that too as he tried to lower his crippled body upon hers. All

191

this Brak saw in an instant, just before he slipped, tumbled, hit the sward, and let out an inadvertent cry.

"One way or another, whore, one way or another, I'll have you," Pom was slathering, his hands everywhere on her. Then he heard Brak's thud and oath. The monstrous head swung around.

Pom's eyes loomed like gray moons. His delicate mouth convulsed.

Brak struggled to all fours. *Get up! Run! Use the knife!* his mind howled. But he was stunned by the fall and exhausted by his battle with the bird, by the burning of his face, by the pain in his eyes where Hektor had gouged. He slumped on the grass again. The dagger slipped out of his fingers.

Pom hitched down to the bottom step, leaving Shana next to naked. Her necklaces had broken somehow. The green stones rained, *click-clack*, around her, an odd sound in contrast to the eerie, faraway singing.

Dazed, Brak once more tried to stand. Tried and could not. Pom seemed a study in unhurried motion, as if he understood that his adversary was weakened and doomed. His tiny child's hands rose upward, extended outward.

Brak knew in the depths of him that one bolt of crystal-white fire from those magical hands would destroy him. He was exposed, a target on the sward. Nowhere to hide and no strength to hide—

Pom's eyes glowed with maniacal fury. His delicate fingers wiggled ever so little, as if he were savoring the killing power that would flash from them.

Brak got to his knees, fumbled for a grip on the knife. Pom screamed some incoherent incantation, extended his arms full length. His fingertips lit with crystal brilliance—

Shana threw herself down the steps to attack him as the sound like a great bell pealed. She was a wild thing, hair flying, arms grappling Pom's legs at the instant the crystal-white fire leaped from his fingertips. Off balance, he fell sideways.

Brak rolled frantically to avoid the bolt. But Pom's hands were flying up now, aimed at the pink and amber heavens. With a furious crackling, crystal-white fire raced for the clouds, trailing smoke, sizzling—

Dissipating.

On his feet, facing his last clean chance, Brak the barbarian flung his throwing hand back, then forward.

The dagger flew fast and true. Pom suddenly doubled over at the middle. He was painfully if not deeply wounded.

Pom tore at the handle sticking twisted into his threadbare robe. Brak could do no more this moment. He slumped down in total exhaustion, to let death come if it would.

Back in the hedges many golden metal birds began to shrill, as if sensing injury to their master. Pom sank to his knees, his huge, distended eyes growing ever more milky. *I haven't killed him,* Brak thought. *I have no more strength. But I haven't killed him.*

Shana's bare limbs gleamed. Pom toppled onto his side. The girl crawled on top of him, pried the dagger from his fingers and cut his throat.

Silence.

The faraway singing suddenly held a mournful note. All the metal birds stilled. Pom lay on his side on the white steps below the little temple where the lamp guttered in the wind. Blood poured out the mouth in his neck to blacken and dampen his robes.

Shana raised her head. Her face looked numb. Her hair hung in straggles. Just a few rags of blouse clung to her breasts.

Brak sucked air. Breathing hurt. Feebly he raised his hand to signal the girl that he was alive. As he lay on the sward, alive and vaguely grateful of that, he suddenly grew sick with a new despair.

They were trapped in an enchanted land, with no way of returning.

Presently he crawled to the girl. It was a journey of torment, but he made it. He held the girl's body in his arms. They huddled together, saying nothing, the only sounds their strident breathing.

Without warning the faces of two gods filled the sky above them.

8

Gods with the faces of evil men:

One was fat. Red-bearded. Moon-eyed and gaping. The other was scrawny, scrofulous, with a scar tracing upward from point of chin to left eye, then on across the ruins of an eyesocket that was no more than a mound of puckered white tissue.

The heads overloomed the garden. The mouths worked, as if the gods were speaking to one another. Shana looked long and hard for a moment. Then she went limp in Brak's arms.

He clenched his teeth against hysteria and stared up at the god-heads. Around them, as they filled half the sky, he saw strange, dark, pulsing spiked halos—shafts of grayness radiating from behind their heads. Within these shafts of halo danced things he half recognized. He was too numb, too hurt and fearful to fully understand the meaning of the specters and what he glimpsed around their heads.

The black sward began to undulate. Began to ripple gently, heave upward, sink down. The hedgerows began to quake and crack.

In an instant the rippling of the earth became more violent. The sky darkened. The spikes behind the heads of the gods grew long and large. The distant singing became minor-key, harsh.

Hedges began to uproot. Great earthballs were torn loose as the land dropped away suddenly beneath them. Brak heard a fearsome cracking, turned—

The elegant white temple swayed, its pillars grinding at their foundations. Even as he watched, a long crack zigzagged upward through the heart of one of the pillars, then raced sideways in two directions to shear the pillar in half. The temple roof buckled.

Chunks of stone tore loose from it, falling to the interior. The lamp went out. Another pillar crumbled in great pieces. One came thundering down toward Brak and the unconscious girl.

He drove himself, harried himself until he found strength to drag her up across his shoulder and stagger down the shallow steps beginning to break apart beneath him. His foot nearly went into a crevass that opened in the earth.

He reached the sward, barely able to stand because the earth was heaving up and down with terrible quakes. The pink and amber sky seemed to be collapsing, falling down upon them, and still the faces of the gods remained looming over all.

Peculiar faces, those, he thought in an almost dream-like moment. Sullen and strangely witless. Coarse peasant faces—

Peasant faces.

The garden of Pom split apart, fissures racing in every direction. One opened under Brak's crotch, so that one foot was on either side.

He flung his weight leftward, teetered with both feet on the edge. Both hands on Shana's bare back, he wrenched himself violently hard, wrenched over and away from the gaping wound in the ground, from which foul odors arose. The hedgerows thrust up every which way, total carnage. The sky grew darker moment by moment. Back in their maze the golden metal birds beat their wings.

Brak's vision began to darken too. He knew full well that this might be the end of his life. Yet he also knew that those strange, looming god-faces were a link to one last chance. If only he weren't so head-weary, so bone-weary! If only he could understand how and why he might save himself and the girl from the darkening holocaust of noise and shuddering earth—

The little temple collapsed upon itself, block crashing on block, pillar on pillar, total ruin.

Several sections rolled down and fell into the cracks in the earth and made no sound thereafter, as if the cracks had no bottoms. Brak breathed like a terrified animal, huddling with Shana in the middle of a patch of heaving sward, staring up dumbly at the two gods.

Peasant faces.

Darker grew the garden; darker. But in the spikes behind the heads of the gods Brak saw a smear of dull orange. As of fire. As of fire in—in a place he should recognize, if only he weren't so weary.

Shana moaned against his shoulder. Terror worked in her even though her mind was blanked by unconsciousness. Brak huddled and snarled and watched the chaos, the grinding, roaring destruction all around him. Time was all but gone.

Peasant faces. Peasant faces staring down from—where? At what? *PEASANT FACES*—

And then, as the tiny cosmos of the garden wracked itself in noise and ruin, as the final moments of destruction roared up in a crescendo of grinding masonry, splitting earth, crashing foliage, Brak the barbarian laughed in a supreme madness. Surely what he understood, what he hoped, was just that—madness. Yet he knew no other way now. And madness was better than accepting this blind, furious death of crashing stone and gutted earth.

Struggling upright, he shot his hand high—*and touched the red beard of the god in the sky.*

Brak wound his fingers deep in the beard, and held on.

The god squealed.

The god tugged, pulled. Brak held on, held on, that one fist wound in long, tangly red hair—

Suddenly, Shana on his shoulder, he felt himself lifted.

He rose up from the heaving earth; up, away from the wracked garden, as if propelled or hauled by some magical force. Upward he rose, toward the faces of the gods.

Once he glanced down. The garden was growing smaller. He thought he saw the steps leading to the little temple break completely apart, and the corpse of Pom the wizard disappear down a long, endless fissure to the bottom of—where?

Everything blinked out.

9

THE FIRST THING Brak heard was a yowl of rage.

In other circumstances the sound might have had a certain com-
icality about it. He let go of a weight on his shoulder, heard something strike softly. Shana, falling—

Sick with nausea, he opened his eyes.

He found himself standing in the cottage of the woodsman, his
hand tangled in the red beard of a god.

No, not a god. Just an immense, sinister-looking, moon-eyed man
in rude clothes; a man who was cursing in a vile way even as he
tried to pull away from Brak's hand.

Through swimming eyes Brak saw the cottage door standing
open. Rain poured in. Behind him he heard the fire pop. He com-
prehended the orange light he had seen in the halos as he looked
back from the garden of Pom to—here.

The other man held Pom's intricately stitched silk. It was torn in
several places. The man had one strip of it tied around his forehead,
an improvised bandana.

These were not gods but only woodland ruffians. The kind of men
Shana had spoken about—

"Shana?"

He called her name wildly, found her lying at his feet, all but
naked. He wiped his palm across his face. The skin hurt horribly,
burned when the gold bird burst. The garden of Pom had heaved
and shaken because—the barbarian did not understand *why*, only
how—because these wandering looters had stolen upon the cottage
and picked up the first and only item of apparent value: Pom's silk.

Why the woodsmen hadn't been propelled into the garden, he

did not know. Perhaps because they had merely handled the silk instead of standing upon it. He was too tired to grapple fully with such an occult mystery, only knowing that by tugging the god's beard at the last instant had he somehow kept the link to reality unbroken, and pulled himself, and Shana, back from the neverland within the cloth—

The scrawny robber with one eye made the sign against evil and backed off, letting the torn silk fall. He clawed at a long curve-bladed knife stuck in his belt.

"Where do you come from?" he said through yellow stump teeth. "Where?"

"A naked gel—a wild man who just appears, pop!—they're demons!" exclaimed the other, moon-eyes redbeard. Brak wondered if he were going to faint. At any time the two would have been formidable adversaries. There was no hint of softness in them. He couldn't hope to fight them in his condition. All he could do was take advantage of their terror. Force himself to lean over, seize a leg of the overturned table. It used almost all his strength to break it off and brandish it—

But that was all that was needed. Shrieking, the two brigands fled from the cottage. A moment later their horses thundered away in the rain.

Half blind with pain, Brak bent, picked up the tatters of the silken garden of the wizard and flung them onto the embers on the hearth. Instantly foul black billows of smoke rolled forth.

The smoke filled Brak's mouth and stung his eyes. The stench was of the pit.

He shoved his hip against the broken table, tilted it, *crash,* half in and half out of the fireplace. He waited until the wood caught. Then he picked up Shana, and her precious carry-bag, and his broadsword—cooled now—and stumbled from the cottage.

As he staggered down the weedy bank toward the foaming river, he heard a crackling behind. The cottage was beginning to burn.

He fell, slid, grabbed weeds to stop himself, crawled back up through the mud to the girl. He cradled her as best he could to protect her from the rain and cold and dark. Numb, he saw and heard nothing more.

10

THE MEADOW WAS warm, the grasses waving and deep. Brak was a long while in kissing Shana one last time.

Finally they rose. Brak rearranged the lion hide about his middle. Behind them, smudgy with color on the horizon, was the rim of the woodland from which they had emerged after several days of journeying along the track. But they did not look that way. Rather, they turned toward a crossroad marked with a signpost showing two directions.

The sun was high and hot, the meadow abuzz with insects as they left it and paused at the junction. In the distance, along the left-hand branching, men and women were haying in a field. A dog yapped near a homestead. A rude cart driven by an old man approached from that direction.

Clad in clothing taken from the carry-bag, the girl was combing her hair free of meadow grass. She looked quite lovely, Brak thought. With some reluctance, he nodded at the right fork of the road.

"That's my way to the south, you say?"

"Aye, Brak. The other way's to Thenngil, and my cousin's farm." She touched him. "I'll not ask to go with you, because you're not a man to travel with another for long."

"And I'll not ask you to go, because then I might not."

Awkwardly he bent and cupped her chin, and kissed her. He looked long into her eyes, remembering the heat of their morning in the meadow, and their nights huddled under blankets back along the track in the gloomy wood, from which, it had seemed several times, they might never emerge.

"Say this for the crazed wizard," remarked Brak with a tenderness that surprised him. "He had an eye for a fair face."

She leaned up to give him another kiss. He knew a pang of regret, a moment's hesitation. Then the song of Khurdisan began to sing in his ears, like a woman's song, but more sweetly than that which he had heard in Pom's unclean garden.

The old fellow driving the cart reached the junction. He gave them an unfriendly stare as he went by. Shana smiled. It did no good. So Brak scowled. That sent the old duffer on his way hastily.

Shana picked up her carry-bag and began to walk along the left-hand road. She waved once, then went on. Her step was sure, her head high, her deep red hair bright in the sunshine. Good. The memories might not be too somber, then. She might dream nightmares of the garden-in-the-cloth, but perhaps she would kiss someone again sometime, and laugh, and even bear strong sons. Good.

His pony had been gone when he woke on the riverbank that morning, to find the woodsman's cottage reduced to smoking rubble. But he didn't mind walking. The sun felt fine on his naked shoulders, and the soothing paste Shana had put on his seared cheeks and the clawed places on his forehead had begun to heal the skin.

He whistled a low, tuneless melody. His yellow braid and the lion tail bobbed in rhythm. He flung his broadsword up across his huge shoulder, point backward, and as he marched south the metal caught the sun and flashed.